Assassin's Fall

Assassin's Fall

ANGELA STEED

Black Lyon Publishing, LLC

ASSASSIN'S FALL
Copyright © 2009 by ANGELA SMEAL

Our books may be ordered through your local bookstore or by visiting the publisher:

www.BlackLyonPublishing.com

Black Lyon Publishing, LLC
PO Box 567
Baker City, OR 97814

This is a work of fiction. All of the characters, names, events, organizations and conversations in this novel are either the products of the author's vivid imagination or are used in a fictitious way for the purposes of this story.

ISBN-10: 1-934912-17-4
ISBN-13:   978-1-934912-17-1
Library of Congress Control Number: 2009926222

COVER MODEL: David McQuisten

Written, published and printed in
the United States of America.

Black Lyon Contemporary Romance

To the amazing women in my life who love to sing eighties rock songs with me, complain about everything in the world with me, sew a mean stitch after a day at the fabric store, draw wonderful pictures, and keep me young at heart with endless tea parties.

Chapter 1

Haley Branson had reached for him on that dark, dreadful night. Under the deafening sound of the helicopter's propellers, she begged him not to let go of the rope, but he did.

If she hadn't seen it with her very own eyes, she would never have believed he was dead. But they executed him, point blank in the chest, as her partners pulled her into the helicopter safely. She'd screamed for them to let her go, to help her save him, but they told her it was too late. He was gone.

For almost a year he'd been her partner in crime and in her arms. Frank Crew, the tall blond, blue-eyed morsel of a man had been one of the most remarkable she'd ever met. He was too smart for his own good and she openly accused him of it, telling him it would somehow get him into trouble, but never did she imagine it would cost him his life.

She became the shrew of her small group of jewel thieves. At least it's what she believed as she sat in silence across the swimming pool watching her partners enjoy lunch beneath a colossal umbrella talking about their newest job. They were only five, but a lethal combination in a deadly criminal organization.

In small framed sunglasses and a black bikini, Haley lay back on the lawn chair soaking in the rays of the L.A. sun. Her long black hair, still damp from the dip she'd taken in the pool just minutes before, began to curl around her shoulders all the way down to her midriff.

She watched her boss walk through the French patio doors of the thirty room mansion and gracefully walk down the steps. Chase Elwin, an intelligent, soft-spoken Englishman with over-the-shoulder auburn hair and big blue eyes that pierced the souls of everyone watching, including her. Deadly in all aspects—looks, power, and of course, whimsical charm that swept everyone off their feet.

He'd taken her in when she was fifteen just after she held him by knifepoint to steal his money. As a gang member and drug runner for one of the nastiest dealers in L.A., she found his soft friendly voice terribly intoxicating. He convinced her to leave the streets and go home with him—but of course not without payment.

He instructed her to work for him training in the ways of an assassin, a code of violence that she was ultimately used to but despised more than anything. But it was better than the life she left behind. With him, she'd found love, family, something she'd never known before. He played like an older brother, respectful, friendly, but overly protective. But he became like a father as more and more, he began to worry about her. And as his worry grew, her part in their performances grew smaller.

"Listen up." Chase gathered everyone's attention from their lunch as he stood at the end of the table. Like clockwork, they set their forks down and gave him their complete attention.

Haley crossed her legs and closed her eyes. The heat from the sun made her body sweat, and another dip in the pool was inviting. But for now, she'd wait until Chase was finished with his typical morale speech.

"Sara," Chase continued, mildly beaming at the young girl. "Your piloting was impeccable during the last operation, young lady."

Sara ran her slender fingers through her short brown hair. Her green eyes sparkled in ambitious gloating. She knew she was good. Graduating from one of the most prestige flight academies in the Air Force, she'd left the military with honors. How she got into crime was beyond anyone's guess.

"I have to say." Chase walked around the table, placed his hands on her shoulders and gently squeezed, "when I heard you flew the Dragon sideways through the canyon, I was rather amused, but I believe I'm happy I missed such excitement."

She smiled brilliantly as the others looked on. She was definitely the kid of the group, cocky but rather diligent when it came to her duties.

He squeezed her shoulders again before he let go of her and walked back around to the front of the table. "I have some news and I won't leave you in suspense. We have a new body joining our group."

Haley immediately took hold of her sunglasses and balanced them on the end of her nose, eyeing Chase curiously. It had been a long time since she'd heard those words. Frank had been their last hire, and she'd hoped there would be no more. In fact, Chase promised.

He glanced over at her knowing his information would gather her attention abruptly. He smiled, then continued his announcement.

"Shane Sin is your next navigational expert. He's trained in martial arts, can take out someone with a M200 at twenty-five hundred meters, and has proven effective in stealth missions."

He turned his head toward the house and let out a shrill whistle. One of his bodyguards dressed in dark sunglasses made his way down the stone steps of the patio. Carrying a black case in his right hand, he looked all business as usual. Here came the plans for the next heist, but all eyes weren't on the case.

Haley suddenly sat up, taking off her sunglasses as she watched a dark-haired man walk down the steps behind him. He was cool, strutting casually with a smirk on his perfectly chiseled face and hands in the pockets of his black dress slacks. His white T-shirt clung to his broad, muscular chest and his bronze arms popped beautifully out of the sleeves.

With a shiver, she watched him come to stand beside Chase. Cockiness shined on him as he took off his sunglasses and greeted the group with a nod.

"Let me introduce everyone." Chase nodded his head, greeting Shane promptly. "We'll start with Jordan."

Jordan blushed mildly when he heard his name. Salt and pepper mingled in with thick lustrous long strands of hair. Wearing a large blue flower print shirt, he looked like a tourist on a Hawaiian vacation.

"Jordan has magic fingers and a genius mind for coding software on the whim. He's our network hacker and is also brilliant with any... electronic gadgets of sorts."

Shane greeted him with a quick nod as Chase winked slyly at Sara. "Sara's our pilot, and a damn good one. She flies the Dragon, as you see there on the lawn."

Chase pointed to the black helicopter sitting on the green grass beyond the pool. A long red dragon was painted down the side of it like an ominous living beast ready to be summoned.

"That's an HH-60 Seahawk," Sara said. "I pulled him from the military dumpster and nursed him back to health myself. I've modified him to be a top rate attack helicopter." Her eyes seemed to glaze with pleasure. "He can fire fifteen hundred rounds in three seconds and carry up to eighteen hellfire missiles. If he was a man, I'd do so many wicked things to him."

Chase tossed her a humble glance. "That's our little grease monkey. All shop talk, and I don't understand a bit of it. If you're finished with your maintenance, I suggest putting him up before he's spotted, hmm?"

"Yeah, yeah," she said, biting her nails and blushing. "It's nice to meet you, Shane."

"Nice to meet you, too," Shane replied, his deep raspy voice carrying to Haley's ears.

Haley could see plain as day Sara was already completely infatuated with him. That's just how she was—knee-deep in ignorant lust when it came to men, especially the good looking ones.

"Diggs is our equipment specialist," Chase said turning Shane's attention to the tall, overly muscular black man with a large Cuban cigar hanging out of his mouth. "Any heavy lifting or firepower necessary, he's the one to go to."

"I only have two rules," Diggs said. "Number two, don't mess with my guns and we'll work fine together."

"What's number one?" Shane asked curiously.

Holding the cigar between his teeth, he widened his gritty grin and answered, "Don't mess with my guns."

"Michael." Chase sighed. "This man is our brilliant scientist. He can concoct a poison to make someone's life a living hell before they die, but can conjure an antidote to bring them back from the dead... even after they've been buried, if that makes any sense. He's bloody frightening sometimes, but very important to our missions."

With large dark eyes behind some rather bulky framed bifocals, Michael eyed Shane smugly. The corners of his mouth rose higher than the rest of his straight pursed lips, but when he showed his teeth, he looked as harmless as a mouse.

"Finally we have Trevor." Chase gazed down at him. The frown on Trevor's face showed he wasn't interested in bringing in someone new to the group. "He's our fearless and quite serious leader. He's a combatant, hand to hand and with any weapon of his choosing. He thinks on his feet and is quick to move when time permits."

"Hello," Shane said, holding out his hand for him to shake. Seeing Trevor wasn't interested in the slightest, he retracted and folded his arms over his chest.

"Now that you've met the group, let's discuss the plans for the mission," Chase said, taking the briefcase from the bodyguard's grasp.

"Wait." Shane noticed Haley who had just dove into the deep end of the pool. "What about her?"

Chase sighed as he watched her resurface and swim toward the shallow end. "I'll introduce her to you later. But then again," he paused as the group let out a few chuckles. "There's no time like the present."

Chase motioned Shane toward the edge of the pool as bets were being placed at the table. He led him toward her just as she stepped up out of the water.

Refreshed, Haley grabbed a towel off the chair and began to dry herself as Chase and Shane came to stand before her. She scowled, just enough to show her irritation to the newcomer.

"Shane," Chase said nervously. "This is Haley. She's trained in martial arts as well. She's fast, confident, and can take down ten men before they even know it. If I were you, I'd do whatever she tells you. Beautiful isn't she?"

Haley loved it when he complimented her, although she wasn't happy with him right then. He usually told her everything, but he hadn't mentioned someone new to her. Of course, whatever he said or decided, she went right along with without complaint, no matter what.

"You two will work closely together. So I imagine you should start getting to know each other now." He gave Haley a stern look when he saw her shocked expression. Normally his look would make her smile, but this time she refused. "I've set you and Shane up on the same wing of the house," he continued. "The closer you two are, the better you'll work together."

He walked away on his word and returned to the group at the table. Haley followed him, wrapping her towel around her waist, ignoring the perfect grin Shane gave her as she walked by.

Wanting to protest, she came to stand beside Chase, but his attention rest on the folders he was removing from the briefcase.

"Here's the map for your next hit," he said passing out the folders. "We're going after Amethyst. It's a small run so it should be easy to get inside. Shane mapped it out yesterday and drew it out on the building schematic in front of you."

"I don't think a new recruit should be allowed to do that without our approval, not on his first job," Haley said.

"I agree," Trevor said with a nod.

"I knew you'd have a problem with this, but I went with him myself. He's drawn out a fool-proof plan."

Haley's eyes grew wide. In all the years she'd been with him, he'd never gone on a navigational run, or any of their heists, for that matter.

"Listen." Chase leaned down, palms to the table. "I realize you're all concerned, but trust me, there's no reason to be. I personally hand-picked Shane to be part of the team knowing he's very much like all of you. You'll just have to trust me on this."

"Then when do we go?" Haley asked as she sat down in an empty chair at the table. Chase always had her trust, so she thought nothing more about it, at least for now.

"Your eagerness is noted my dear," Chase replied. "We're scheduled for next weekend. That gives you nine days to go over the plan." He stood up straight. "I'll leave you to your discussion, for I have pressing matters to tend to."

Chase turned around and left for the house. Haley watched him intently, glancing at Shane who also watched him leave.

"This looks too easy," Sara chimed.

"It may be a small facility, but that doesn't mean it's going to be easy," Trevor said as he glanced at the map. "According to the specs, the safe is in an underground vault with only one way in and out. I'm sure there'll be security all over it."

"Why the hell are we lifting Amethyst?" Diggs asked, taking his blunt cigar out of his mouth and laying it in the ash tray on the table. "It's garbage, practically worthless."

"It doesn't matter," Trevor answered. "We're not paid to ask questions."

Diggs leaned back in his chair and sighed. "Well as long as we get paid, I don't care if we're stealing baskets of dirty socks."

Haley took her folder from the table and stood up. Her towel came loose and fell from her waist, but when she reached down to pick it up, she met Shane's hand.

With her eyes fixed on his, she stood back up. He handed her the towel, but she didn't return his grin with one of her own.

"I guess we're going to be working together," he said, holding the towel out for her to take.

"I heard." With pursed lips she took the towel from his grasp and started toward the house. The tension in her began to rise impatiently as Shane fell into pace right on her heels. And when they reached the top step of the patio, she couldn't stand it anymore.

"Listen." She stopped immediately, turned around, and glared at him, trying to keep her mind off his gorgeous long lashes and the most beautiful muddy eyes she'd ever seen. "I don't like being followed."

"Whether you like it or not, we're going to be working together. So you might as well cut out the tough girl act and try to get along with me."

If it were possible eye-color could change by a swing of mood, hers would turn from her normal sky blue to a deep fiery red. As she lay her folder down on the small stone bistro table near the steps, her lips curved.

"You have a lot of nerve," she said. "If you know what's good for you, you'd shut your mouth and back off."

She glowered, ignoring the way he flexed his muscles—preparing for a fight. As he rubbed his hands together, she kicked her sandals off beneath the bistro chair, ultimately ready to go head to head with him.

"If you fight me, you'll just end up losing," he said with a chuckle.

"We'll see about that," she replied as she began to walk around him. "So are you game? Or are you chicken?"

"I'll play." His smile broadened as he too kicked off his shoes next to hers. "Give me your best shot."

She watched him closely as they began a dance around each other. They were like boxers in the ring, each searching for a vulnerable spot before the first punch was thrown.

It'd been a long while since she felt like this, no holds barred.

And she began to enjoy this little test of skills. The only question now was who would make the first strike, and then he suddenly stopped in an open stance—perfect.

Haley quickly struck his jaw with her right fist, knuckles out. A punch like this would have made her fight trainer proud, but then he'd complain she'd held back giving her opponent a chance to strike back. That was the idea.

Shane rubbed his jaw as he laughed, raspy and deep-growled. It sounded playful at first, but grew curiously arousing as his voice became serious.

"Was that your best?" he asked as he shook off the pain, lowering his brows. "You can do better than that."

"You talk too much," she said as she quickly jumped into the air. She pulled her body around, attempting a swift kick to his face, but he blocked it with his arm, catching her ankle in mid-air.

Before she realized what happened, he'd shoved her face into the ground and held her arm behind her back. It was painful, but not unmanageable.

"You're too slow," he said, lifting her hand slightly upward, causing her a little distress. "Give up?"

"Never," she replied.

It took all the muscles in her stomach and legs to push away from his hold as she threw her leg back and hit him hard just below his ear. It hurt enough for him to let go of her hand, giving her time to lift her body with her arms, and flip to her feet.

She caught him off-guard and flung her curved arm toward his stunned face, but he impressively blocked it as if he had some sort of extra-sensory perception to her moves. But he didn't see the fist she made with her other hand, and she quickly hit him in the chest.

It was a sneaky move, and one on a reflex to take the breath away from him. He let out a pained gasp, but she wasn't about to quit until he was down on the ground begging for her to stop. He'd started this fight, and she would end it right now.

She hit him in the ribs with her clenched fist, causing him another painful gasp. She grabbed him by the arm and swiftly flipped him forward making him land flat on his back. She sat down on his stomach, and held her arm across his neck, blocking the wind from his trachea.

She breathed hard with an overconfident smile as he stared up at her with pitiful eyes. He couldn't breathe. And although she'd love to continue her choke hold on him until he passed out cold, she let up.

"You lose," she said.

"Have I?" he asked, struggling with his voice. "You're way too self-assured to believe it'd be that easy to take me down."

As his cocky grin returned, hers diminished. During her premature gloating, he'd reached across her back. He grasped her arm, and with a quick jerk and shove, threw her off.

She tumbled down the steps, holding her arms to her face as she fell. She winced as the concrete scraped her legs and arms until she reached the bottom near the group watching the fight intently.

Trevor stood up, an aggravated frown lingering on his stern face. He started toward her, but was stopped by her infuriated glance.

"That's enough, Haley," Trevor spoke in a low voice.

"Stay out of this," she said as she rose to her feet and turned her attention to Shane, who had already made his next move.

His foot quickly came toward her forcing her to lean to the side, just barely avoiding a blow to her face. She backed away from him in a defensive stance, blocking each punch he threw at her as they moved down the side of the pool toward the lawn.

"Have you had enough?" he asked, throwing a straight punch at her neck.

"Enough?" she breathed hard as she moved in time to miss his attack. "I'm just getting started."

Shane laughed as he threw another straight punch, but this time she ducked and rolled to the side. She scrambled up the retaining cinder block wall that led to the enormous backyard with him on her heels.

She gracefully jumped off to the other side and landed in the grass, finding the opportunity to switch to offense. Sweat beaded her brow and dripped down her nose as she turned to face him.

"You're pretty good," she said. "But your moves are messy."

"Speak for yourself. I'm wearing dress-slacks."

"Excuses ..."

He suddenly closed the distance between them with a quick twist of his leg, but unfortunately left him completely vulnerable to one of the best places to cause a man immense pain. He saw his mistake and realized it was too late to avoid her next move.

Haley ducked and slid beneath him. She sent an uppercut punch straight into his groin, twisted her wrist enough to send him spiraling to the ground writhing in tremendous pain.

Before he could recover, she straddled his neck and squeezed his head between her thighs. The last time she'd done this to a man, she'd hospitalized him. And if she didn't let up soon, she'd probably do the same thing to Shane, who didn't look like he could take much more.

"I win again," she said, breathing hard watching his eyes roll slightly as he gasped for breath.

She hesitantly loosened her grip, hoping he'd stay down this time. "Give up?" she asked in a condescending tone.

"Never," he gasped and then quickly grabbed her ankles. He forced her legs open removing the strain from his throat. He found his breath as he turned her over and quickly moved overtop of her. And with his body pressed hard against hers, she was the one who couldn't breathe.

"Get off me!" she gasped, finding him rather dismayed. His face was red from nearly being choked to death and the veins prominently lined his temple.

"Not until you say you give," he said, panting.

"Never," she replied hatefully, struggling to free herself, but he had her locked down and wasn't about to let up.

"Say it." He wrapped his hands around her wrists.

"I won't!"

He brought her arms up over her head and pinned them to the ground. He carefully pulled his body up so she could take a breath, but he held her legs down with his knees, causing extreme discomfort.

"You're stubborn," he said running his eyes down to her lips, and then his infuriating look turned into a mischievous glance.

Knowing he'd regret it, he leaned down and kissed her on the mouth. It wasn't the kind of kiss to bring a woman to her knees, but a hard-pressed one, as if their lips played in combat themselves.

Strangely, Haley liked it, but not enough to let him get away with it. She lowered her chin and pulled her head up, hitting him hard on the nose, enough to get him to move off her and fall to the side.

She quickly leapt to her feet, only to fall back to the ground. It felt like electric shooting through her legs, leaving her immobilized with horrible pain. "What did you do to me?" she cried out.

"It hurts, doesn't it?" He chuckled over her furious glare and then sighed. "There are nerves in your legs that when just enough pressure is applied can cause paralyzing pain. It's just enough to keep you here for another minute or two while I make my getaway."

He stood up and wiped blood from his nose with the back of his hand. He glanced at the bright red stain and then gave a short laugh through his mouth.

"In all my years of fighting, I've never once let anyone purposely hit me. You should consider it a compliment."

"You're full of yourself," Haley spat as she struggled to move.

The intense pain began to fade, but it still stung like crazy working from her toes to her thighs. "Just make it stop," she moaned almost in tears.

Shane crouched down beside her. He stared into her glittering eyes and then grabbed hold of her leg just above the knee. He squeezed hard at first and then gently ran his hands slowly up, massaging as he went until they were around her upper thigh, a little too close for comfort. He squeezed one more time before quickly releasing his grasp sending a strange tingling sensation through her leg, and then the pain immediately went away.

Haley moved her knee back and forth as she breathed a relieving sigh. "The other one," she demanded.

Shane stepped over her and quickly reached down and released her other leg, stopping the pain completely. She glared as he helped her to her feet.

"I'm sorry," he apologized as they began walking back up to the house. "I didn't mean to humiliate you in front of your team."

Watching as the disappointed men paid Sara, who'd obviously bet on Shane winning the fight, Haley shook her head. She stepped up the patio stairs with him beside her.

"If I'd not let up on you twice—well, I wouldn't apologize for humiliating you."

As he walked behind her down the hallway of the house, she could sense his stare. She couldn't help but like him even though he'd won their fight. But then again, it was probably the reason she found him terribly likable. And though she wanted to continue liking him, she couldn't let him get close enough for her to care.

She stopped at her bedroom door as he stopped at the one across from hers and unlocked it. He opened it wide and then came to stand before her.

"He gave you that room?"

He nodded, folding his arms over his chest. "Right across from yours."

"I'll have to talk to him about your arrangements. I'm sure he'd let you move to a room at the end of the hall in another wing."

"Away from you?" he asked, arching his brow.

"That's the idea."

She twisted the knob on the door and opened it wide. The sun beamed generously through a white flowing sheer curtain in the open patio door.

"Nice room," Shane said as he gazed at the four posted bed, fit for a king, or queen for that matter.

"I'm going to shower and change." She glanced at the large metal framed clock on the wall. "We're all meeting for dinner at six. I'll see you then."

She closed the door on him slowly thinking something was definitely amiss with him. But in time she'd learn what it was—possibly with some snooping.

As she closed the door and walked to the bed, she inspected the scrapes on her arms. These were going to be unsightly at dinner. Chase's boss had decided to come, and he was meticulous for noticing the small things, especially when it came to her.

Chapter 2

"There I was," Richard said holding out his hands, looking down at them as he reenacted a scene in his story. "Holding the most beautiful diamonds I'd ever seen. I had no idea what to do with them. On one side of me, the cops were telling me I'd be a free man if I just handed them over and testified against my boss who just happened to be standing on the other side of me. Mr. Yoshino wasn't one to be trifled with. His men pointed their machine guns at me, shouting if I didn't move now they'd start shooting. I almost pissed my pants."

Haley noticed Shane hanging on his every word. Granted, Richard Boman was a wonderful storyteller. Sometimes she wondered if he exaggerated just a bit.

"So, you know what I did?" he asked Shane with a curve of his lips, making the wrinkles in his skin look worse than when he frowned. "I stuffed them inside my pocket, flipped off the cops, flipped off Mr. Yoshino, and then walked straight off the pier into the icy water of the lake."

He belted out a laugh that boomed through the dining room. The rest of the team, including Shane, laughed along with him, as a courtesy maybe, but Haley remained straight-lipped and unenthused.

Chase lowered his brows, motioning her to join in before Richard caught her with a smirk on her face, but it was too late.

"Haley, my dear," Richard said, catching her attention. "What's wrong with you tonight? You look as though you've lost your best friend again."

She hated when he brought up Frank. Somehow she thought maybe he got enjoyment out of seeing her writhe in unwanted memories. Or quite possibly he was keeping up his act, hiding from everyone in the room the reality of what their relationship really was.

It had only been a few weeks since he'd forced her into an unthinkable corner, one she desperately wished she could get out of. To watch Chase closely, reporting any unauthorized operations was easy, but unnecessary.

She'd found nothing of the sort, but for some reason, they still believed he held back some of the stolen jewels for his own monetary purposes. And then her job took a huge turn from spy to assassin.

Richard ordered her to kill him, assassinate him, or however she was allowed to play the words. It was supposed to happen after their next heist, and she struggled with the idea. No matter how loyal she was to the organization, she just didn't think she could do it.

She'd thought about disappearing, but she couldn't go off and leave Chase to die by someone else's hands. But if she stayed and disobeyed her orders, they would both assuredly wind up dead.

"Haley," Richard gathered her attention again. "Frank would be wondering what was wrong if he saw you with such a droopy expression."

"Who's Frank?" Shane asked, glancing over at her curiously.

Aggravated over Richard's condescending tone and all the attention on her, she pushed her chair out and stood up. "Excuse me."

Shane watched her leave out the double doors to the covered patio. He could tell Richard hit a sensitive spot by the sorrowful look on her face. And by the look on his old wrinkled mug, he enjoyed making her feel that way.

"Frank was our last navigator," Trevor said in a concerned voice. "He died on one of our heists after he was caught. She's supposed to be the last person in, but he insisted she go first that night. So she blames herself." Trevor looked out the window at her with solemn eyes. "I think she cared a lot about him."

Shane's eyes widened. "I had no idea, otherwise I wouldn't have said ..."

"Don't worry about it." Chase interrupted. "It's time for her to move on."

"It's been a year," Sara said, rolling her eyes. "She's been a real pain to put up with."

"Sara." Chase gave her a disappointed glare.

"You know," she said, leaning back in her chair. "I really don't care anymore. I'm sick of hearing about it. She shouldn't have fallen for him in the first place. It's just not right to get involved like that with anyone in the group."

"But you are all involved with each other," Richard chimed in, offering his opinion. "I am ashamed that the stars of the organization have such animosity toward each other over something as trivial as this. You should support her in her time of grief. Comfort her, console her," he stated with his unruly eyes on her. "Let her know she's desired."

Shane couldn't help but glare. Though he'd thought him an interesting man before, his hypocrisy was less than respectful. He could also see the yearning behind his eyes.

"You don't get it," Sara argued. "We supported her. But it's been long enough for her to get over it." Realizing she was being a bit hasty, she sighed and returned to her usual slump. "I don't want to talk about her anymore. She gets enough attention as it is."

Shane watched Sara leave the table, followed by Diggs. They seemed to be an inseparable pair. And as far as he could tell, they were involved in some odd, secretive way.

Jordan sat for a moment longer. But seeing nobody was chatting anymore, he left to join the other two at the bar on the other side of the dining room wall.

Shane felt a bit awkward being left alone with the other four. They seemed to have their own tensions.

"Excuse me." Shane stood up and dismissed himself from the table.

He walked out onto the patio and breathed in a sigh of relief. It felt good to be away from what seemed to be a fight waiting to break out.

Haley sat on a patio chair in the dark, watching him lean against the stone banister. She hoped he wouldn't see her, but he glanced her way.

"Hey," he said as he walked over to her.

She rested her ankle on her knee and stared off into the dark. Maybe if she didn't acknowledge him, he'd go away.

"How're the scrapes?" he asked, leaning back against the

banister.

"I've felt worse."

"I never meant to open old wounds ..."

"Don't apologize," she interrupted, lifting her voice over his. "Frank tried to be a hero and failed, that's all."

"You were in love with him though. It had to hurt to see him die right in front of you."

She felt warmth in her face. "I wasn't in love with him."

"I'm not going to judge you for having a heart."

"What's with you?" she asked in an aggravated breath. "You've only been here for a day and you're acting like my shrink." She stood up and glared as she walked to the other side of the patio, and folded her arms over her chest.

He chuckled softly and then made his way to her side. He laid his hands on her shoulders and gently squeezed. "I'm sorry. I just feel like we have some sort of connection, kind of like we've known each other forever. And I figured if you needed someone to talk to, I'd listen."

Haley really started to worry now. It was too odd for a man she'd never met before to act like he knew her and stranger yet, care for her.

She tilted her head to the side and gave him a puzzled look. She saw nothing but mystery.

"You know," she said. "I can tell there's more to your hire than just replacement."

He let out a deep raspy laugh, genuinely amused.

"Laugh all you want," she said. "But your act isn't convincing me."

She turned and leaned over the banister, brushing a few long black strands of hair behind her ear. She gazed out across the courtyard spotting the lit-up pool as he leaned in beside her.

"Okay, I'll tell you the truth if you really want to know," he confessed. "Chase was my father's friend."

Haley glanced at him blankly. She could see the solemn look in his eye at the mention of his father. And knowing loss all too well, she sympathized.

"So how did you get involved in the organization?" she asked.

"When my parents died, Chase took me in and sent me to a training facility through the organization. It was kind of like military school, but tougher."

Surprised to hear this, she became suspicious. After all, she would have known Chase had another prodigy besides herself. He had to be lying. And then she wondered if he was really working for Richard, keeping an eye on her, or worse yet, taking over something she most likely couldn't finish.

"Since we're going to be working together, maybe we should get to know each other a little better."

Haley pursed her lips in thought. If Shane was here to do the job she was supposed to do, maybe she shouldn't let him out of her sight.

"What do you have in mind?"

He grinned slyly. "What's on your agenda for tomorrow?"

"I hadn't planned anything."

"What do you say we go somewhere?"

"No," she answered with an arched brow, waiting for a convincing reason.

"I know this guy who runs a skydiving business at the airport."

Her attention suddenly peaked. It seemed it had been years since she'd been out of the mansion to have some fun, and skydiving was right up her alley. And what better way to keep an eye on him, then to get him out of the house—away from Chase.

"He runs the planes every day, so I'm sure it'll be cool with him if we tag along."

She wanted to decline again, but the overwhelming desire to get out made her body ache in excitement. A short smile escaped her lips, though she knew she shouldn't have let it go.

"You're beautiful," he said, elbowing her playfully.

He had to ruin her moment. Yet again, he was trying to get close but the wall she built stood strong as she frowned and walked away. Thankfully, he didn't follow as she made her way to her room.

She opened the door and stepped inside, but when she reached for the light switch, somebody's hand grasped hers tightly.

"Haley," he said in a low grumbling voice. "Leave the light off."

"Richard?"

Her eyes widened. He was in her room, and without permission. The possibility he'd kill her there on the spot ran through her mind, making her tremble slightly. And when he touched her softly on her neck, she shivered.

"My dear," he said, almost in a whisper. "I imagine you're wondering why I'm here."

"Yes sir," she said, keeping deathly still.

The moon shone through the window, giving the man an eerie presence as it reflected off his white thinning hair. The way he touched her, running his cold fingers across her skin made her ill, but she let him do it. She had to.

Silhouettes stood near the window—his bodyguards holding machine guns in their arms as if they were going off to war. Her heart skipped at the thought they were here for her.

"Rest easy," he said as he ran his fingers down her arm and then squeezed her hand gently. "I am only here to give you an update on your mission. I dare not take advantage of such a beautiful woman."

She breathed a sigh of relief. He'd come to her this way before, but never in the presence of his bodyguards. She wondered if maybe he'd become just as afraid of her as she was of what terrible things he could do.

"The job I asked of you," he said. "It's been upped to the priority list. No longer will you wait for word. Instead, you will be rid of the problem as soon as this weekend."

Haley's eyes widened. "How am I supposed to—"

"Listen to me," he said, placing his hands on her shoulders. "I have all confidence in your abilities. Chase must be dealt with."

She watched him as he moved passed her to the bedroom door, wishing she was in another place right now. Of all people he had under his beck and call, why did he have to come to her?

"By the way," he said, turning one last time before he opened the door. "If it isn't finished by Monday, well, I'd hate to see such a lovely young woman beg for her life."

He turned the knob and opened the door. The gleam in his eyes remained as he closed the door leaving her in her horrified state.

She quickly flipped on the light and turned around. The room was empty. As if they were ghosts in the shadows, the bodyguards disappeared.

She massaged her temples as she kicked off her shoes and walked to the small recliner. Sinking down into the cushion, her thoughts began to race.

This was by far the toughest thing she'd ever dealt with. She'd never killed a soul in her years working for the organization, and she didn't want to start.

Chase wasn't stealing from the company. She knew Richard just made that excuse for her. There was something else going on between them.

She could ask Chase about it, but then he'd get suspicious and either flee or face the music. Regardless of what he'd do, they would turn on her, and kill her for betraying them.

She wasn't a coward, so running was out of the question, but she wasn't a fool either. If he'd betrayed them in some way, she needed to know what it was. And it'd be then she'd decide if she truly needed to kill him, or help him escape.

Chapter 3

They took off early before the sun rose above the mountains. It felt good to be out of the dreary mansion and into the coolness of the dawn, knowing this day would be about relaxing and being away from every wrong thing going on.

Dressed in tan shorts and a plain white T-shirt over a navy blue bikini in case they ended up at the beach, Haley was ready to go. She tied her long black hair away from her face and armed her eyes with her favorite dark shades. She met Shane in the horseshoe driveway in front of the house, and they were off.

The sun peeked as they drove up the coastal highway, heading outside the city. With the top hatch off, the wind swirled through the small SUV. She only wished they could keep driving, leaving all evils behind her, but she knew it could never happen—it wouldn't.

Shane glanced at her from time to time. With the morning sun on her bronzed skin, she looked like a glamorous vixen, petite and harmless. And with the pleasant smile she wore as she gazed out the open window, it was hard to believe she was a lethal player in a dirty organization.

"Hungry?" he asked, gathering her attention on him. "There's a small beach front restaurant up here. They have the best omelets around."

She nodded. And as they pulled into the gravel parking lot of the restaurant, the scent of breakfast food wafted into her nostrils. The sensation of hunger grew and her stomach growled.

It had been a long time since she'd been out to eat, especially breakfast. She remembered sitting in a small café in the middle of L.A. with Frank where they ate croissants and drank coffee. They'd been seated uncomfortably near a table of cops peculiarly eyeing them the entire time. It was a strange breakfast, and she wondered how this morning would go with Shane.

He opened the door for her, greeting her with his usual grin. She walked underneath his arm and inside the quaint diner wonderfully decorated with beach paraphernalia. The waitress greeted them and beamed as she led them to a table outside on the deck.

As Haley sat down, she gazed out at the scenery. The sparkling blue ocean beyond a white sandy beach looked marvelous, making her want to paddle out on her surfboard and catch the largest wave.

"It's a beautiful day to go surfing," she said.

"The waves are great here. I come here a lot, or rather I used to before I started working for Chase."

She was surprised he'd told her something as personal as where he hung out. As part of the team, their personal lives were to remain anonymous to each other.

Their breakfast was finally served. Crispy bacon and a large vegetable omelet smelled delightful, and she dug her fork in. It was an odd feeling. Any food she could think of was available at her request at the mansion, but none of it seemed real compared to this. Like a home-cooked meal made just for her, this was just what she needed.

She felt relaxed as she ate. Maybe it was from the really good food, or possibly from the beach atmosphere. Or maybe it was the company.

He watched her intently, always smiling when she glanced at him. It was possible she misunderstood thinking him one of Richard's men, because here, now, he seemed genuine. This was a rather unusual trait for a criminal, especially one within this organization. Most of the guys were weird and kept to themselves, but this one—she caught his eye again—he was different.

His friendly guise suddenly made her feel slightly uncomfortable, considering she'd only known him for a day. But she considered herself a good judge of character, and she began to believe Chase may have actually picked a good partner for her. Of course, the day had only begun, and a lot could happen by the time it was over.

"Tell me about you," he said setting his fork down in his empty plate.

"There's not much to tell," she said, shoving her dish to the edge of the table.

She dabbed her napkin on each corner of her mouth and propped her elbows up on the table. She crossed her legs and glanced out at the ocean, avoiding his curious stare.

"I don't believe you." He chuckled. "I imagine you've seen many things in your lifetime."

She laughed at his comment. "My lifetime?"

"Well, yeah," he replied. "You're what, twenty-five? You've been in the business since you were twelve. I'd say that's a lifetime."

"How'd you know that?" she asked curiously.

"Lucky guess," he said as the waitress picked up their plates.

"Anything else I can get you two?" she asked in a sweet voice.

"No," Haley answered politely.

She watched the waitress walk back inside the building. With lowered brows, she returned her attention to Shane, who was staring out at the ocean.

"Chase told you about me?" she asked, knowing it was true. Chase was the only one to know such things about her time in the organization.

"I won't deny we've discussed your business. But he's only told me bits and pieces, just enough information to be able to work with you without a blind start."

"Well, he must trust you then," she said, though a little aggravated they'd been talking about her behind her back. "What you see is what you get. I don't like making a spectacle of myself. I don't go out to party like the other members of the team. Actually, I prefer a nice quiet corner to sit in. I'm a loner and I'd prefer it to stay that way."

"So what's with you and Trevor?" he asked, folding his arms over the table as he leaned in, intrigued to hear her answer.

"What do you mean?"

"I can tell there's something going on between you and him. Are you involved?"

She suddenly laughed, leaning back in the bench seat. The plastic was cool against her skin, making her shudder slightly.

"No, we're not involved."

"Then who do you talk to? With so much crap on your mind, you must have someone you let loose on."

"You're asking a lot of personal questions."

"It's nothing," he answered, taking her by the hand. "I'm just trying to get you to open up and confide in me. You need someone to trust, and I'm hoping that person will be me."

"Trust is earned. And right now I'm not too sure about you."

"So let me earn it by listening. I want to know everything about you. I want to be there for you when you need someone."

"Wow," she said, finding herself on her feet. "You're crazy if you think I need a hero. This is just a little too much."

She grabbed her purse from the seat and tucked it under her arm. Walking through the restaurant she spotted the waitress at the checkout stand and handed her a fifty dollar bill.

"Keep the change," she told her as she walked out into the parking lot, ignoring Shane's offer to pay the waitress a twenty.

"Thank you." The waitress swooned slightly over the thirty dollar tip.

Shane caught up with Haley before she reached the car. He grabbed her by the arm and swung her around to face him.

"Don't walk away from me," he said, ignoring her perturbed glance as she stood in front of him.

"Let me go before I make you," she growled.

He let go of her arm, but held his stare to hers. If she didn't know any better, she would have thought he wanted her to kick his ass in the middle of the parking lot. And she probably would if there weren't families around them, preparing to go out on the beach for the day.

"Listen," she spoke in a low harsh tone. "Let's just go skydiving and forget the personal talk. That's not why I came."

She found the truck and hopped in. Shane got into the driver's seat and started the engine. He refused to let it go as he pulled back out on the highway. There was nowhere for her to run away now.

"Talk to me," he said, glancing at her, pushing her buttons.

"Shut up," she said.

"I promise what you tell me will only be between us. You have my word."

"Your word doesn't mean anything to me."

"Well, then how about a pinky swear?"

She turned and stared at his hand held up for her. With his pinky stuck up in the air waiting for her to give him hers, he looked like a little smiling boy waiting for candy.

"You've got to be kidding." The cynical tone in her voice matched her look of bewilderment. "Exactly how old are you?"

"Twenty-nine," he answered, still holding up his pinky finger with a wide ear-to-ear grin. "Come on, take it."

"I'm not going to play your games," she said as she looked out the front window at the passing yellow lines on the road.

"Come on," he begged. "Take my pinky."

"No," she felt her lips curving upward.

"Listen," he said placing his hand back on the steering wheel. "I swear to you I'm trustworthy. I can tell you're a good judge of character." He glanced at her briefly. "If that's so, then you should be able to take my hand and give me one of your beautiful smiles by the end of the day."

She turned away, finding herself in thought. He had a sense of humor nobody else around her carried. He was sweet, and at this moment he seemed someone she could trust, but she still had to be wary. He was obviously very close to Chase, and one wrong word could send everything spiraling down around her.

"Fine," she answered as they pulled off the highway and headed toward the small airport near the beach. "I'll take your pinky swear and hold you to it, if you prove to me I can trust you, and that might take awhile."

He laughed heartily at her answer. "Alright, we're finally getting somewhere."

She loved his deep, raspy laugh; it made her feel relaxed and comfortable. She only hoped he wouldn't disappoint her and turn out to be a man out for his own selfish reasons. And she prayed he wasn't a man on a mission from someone higher up in the organization.

◆

The sound of the plane's engine roared in Haley's ears. She made one last tug on the belt around her waist and over her shoulders.

It had been at least six months since her last jump and the adrenaline raced through her, barely able to stand still as she imagined the fall through the perfect sky. Sure, jewel heists were quite the rush to pull off, but skydiving—this was a thrill all in its own. The possibility of the chute not opening was gut-wrenching to think about. The chance of landing in an unwanted destination, the ocean reef, close to power lines, or even on a busy highway was there. This was only part of what made it unbelievably exciting.

"About five more minutes," the pilot yelled back at them. "And we'll be over the target area."

"You're not excited are you?" Shane yelled, enjoying the exhilaration in her eyes. "How long has it been?"

"Six months," she yelled back. "What about you?"

"Two weeks," he replied.

Holding on to the circular strap attached to the ceiling of the plane with one hand, she used the other to position her goggles over her eyes. The pilot quickly pulled the plane upward making her lose her footing, and she slipped right into Shane's arms.

"Hi," he said, holding on to her as the plane leveled off.

She found her balance and stood back up. If she didn't know any better, it was part of the plan to move her closer to him. She opened her mouth to stress her concern, but the pilot's voice interrupted her.

"Okay," he yelled back at them. "Thirty second countdown."

In her mind, she counted backward. As she moved to the open door, Shane followed. She let him hold on to her arm as she stepped out onto the bar. And with a nod she was ready to jump, he let her go.

Diving head first, the wind rushed against her face. As if her very spirit set loose upon the world, she flew through the sky, soaring downward toward the earth far beneath her. She wished she could stop time to have a serious look around, and maybe even take a photograph or two of the ocean or the mountainous terrain.

Breathtaking was the only word to sum it up. It had been too long since she'd felt this way, extraordinarily happy and carefree. But then maybe she never felt this sort of emotion before. If only she could bring the sensations with her when her feet touched the ground, she'd let loose the tough girl and shed tears bottled up inside, but then again, they were almost coming now. Only here could she show her true emotions, at least that's how she felt until she released the chute from the pack and came to a sudden slow down.

As she glided toward the ground, she found Shane close by riding smoothly beneath his bright orange chute. He waved at her.

She couldn't help but laugh at his silly gestures and comments, making her feel like a young, blissful woman, something she'd never quite experienced before. Frank had never made her feel this way. He was never an adrenaline junky like she was, and definitely not at all like Shane who was proving every minute he was more her style.

The landing was perfect. She touched the ground with her feet and caught her balance. Gravity caught up with the chute as it fell on the ground behind her, rustling in the warm breeze.

Shane landed at the same time and gave out a sudden energized yell. Oddly, she laughed and yelled back with her own joyful chant.

She unbuckled the pack and let it slide from her arms as Shane walked over to her. The smile radiating off of him was returned with her own grin.

"I can't get enough of it," he said pulling off his helmet and goggles. "It's more than a rush!"

"I agree," she said as she tied her hair up with the rubber band she'd carried around her wrist. She watched his chest heave as he unzipped his bodysuit, exposing his perfect bare pecks.

Without thinking, she unzipped hers and took it off. Standing in her bikini, she caught him staring at her body.

"It's too hot to be wearing a suit, so I'd appreciate it if you kept your eyes above my chest."

"I'm sorry," he said. "But you're such a beautiful …"

"Whatever," she interrupted, returning to her normal aggravated tone.

"Ah now," he said as they started walking toward the oncoming truck coming to pick them up. "Don't let the rush die."

"I won't. Just keep your compliments to yourself."

He fell into stride beside her as the truck stopped in front of them. She was surprised he didn't have a comeback for her comment. And from the corner of her eye, she could see him sulking.

"Sorry," she said as they climbed into the back of the truck. "I'm just not used to accepting compliments."

"It's okay," he replied. "I normally don't give them."

He stared at her the entire ride back to the airport. The concern in his eyes showed. He was so mysterious.

"Shall we hit the beach?" she asked as they reached the airport. "Maybe we could hit a few waves, do a little sunbathing, and then," she paused, "… go to dinner?"

"I'm stunned." He arched his brows in surprise. "Are you suggesting we go out on a date tonight?"

"No." She shook her head as she hopped out of the truck, amused at his reaction. "We're all meeting again tonight to go over plans."

He hopped out beside her with one quick leap. A look of dismay set across his face when he saw her eyes droop with her thoughts.

"Are you okay?" he asked as they started toward the small terminal.

"Fine," she answered.

He grabbed her hand and stopped her just outside the door. With a quick gentle pull, he turned her around to face him. The serious look on his face made her flinch nervously.

"Have you ever thought about getting out?"

His question was sudden. The seriousness in his voice was as if a completely different person spoke to her. She found it rather alarming.

"Why would you ask me something like that?" she asked, feeling rather awkward. She had to be careful in case he was more involved with her boss than she thought.

"Answer the question," he pleaded, pushing her body back against the wall. "I promise I won't tell anyone. It'll be our secret." She gazed into his eyes. Her heart skipped and adrenaline rushed through her.

"Yes," she blurted, unable to stop herself from answering. It was easier than she thought.

He leaned against her, holding on to her arms. The seriousness suddenly left him, and his playful smile returned. His entire body seemed to let out a sigh of relief that she'd answered him honestly, and she knew then he believed her.

"I knew it," he whispered as he palmed her face.

"You promised," she reminded him as he gently pushed her head back against the window.

"I swear on my own life," he said. "I will never tell. I just needed to hear it from your lips."

With a smooth lean, he parted his mouth over hers. It wasn't like the hard, horrible kiss he gave her when they were fighting, but it was pure, gentle, a mesmerizing kiss that any woman would fall weak over.

He pulled her arms around his neck and reached around her waist. Picking her up off her feet, he pulled at her lips as he walked her toward the glass door of the terminal.

He set her down and pulled away from her. The grin he wore went with him as he opened the door and walked inside, pulling her with him by her hand.

"We should go away together."

She gave him a strange look. "That's a little sudden."

"That may be true," he agreed with a nod, "but I am serious. I'm going to take you away from the mansion for awhile. You need a vacation. What do you say about skiing in the Alps?"

"I'm not a fan of frigid weather."

"Then let's go to Cancun and catch some waves."

He stared down at her, pleadingly, but all Haley could do was shake her head knowing in her heart there would be no way possible, not after the horrible deed she had to carry out for the organization. She opened her mouth to decline, but he quickly interrupted.

"Lunch then?" he asked as he finally greeted the impatient woman behind the desk. Obviously she'd seen their public display of affection outside the window by the way she scowled.

"Lunch is good," was all Haley could say as she watched his warm smile melt the scowling woman into putty.

Chapter 4

"There's so much detail in this." Trevor shook his head in disbelief. "I know it's a smaller building than what we're used to, but damn." He glanced up from the detailed map. "This is unusual."

"How long have you been staking the place out?" Diggs asked as he puffed on his cigar.

Shane glanced at Chase, and then at Haley who sat near the patio door inspecting the plan. She'd been eyeing him all night, and he'd even been lucky to catch a faint smile from her.

"Honestly," Shane sighed at the five lingering eyes watching him carefully. "I used to work security for these people. It was a very long time ago, but I still know a few people inside that tell me nothing ever changes."

Trevor chuckled. "It figures."

Ignoring Trevor's condescending tone, Shane went on. "Regardless of my knowledge, it's still going to be tricky. There are no vents to crawl through, so moving in silence won't be an option. It's all guns blazing ... so to speak."

Shane looked at Michael, who'd kept quiet as usual throughout dinner. It seemed the guy never said a word to anyone, which made him seem more menacing than what the rest of the team made him out to be.

"Michael," Shane said, gathering his large eyes on him. "You can concoct a sleep agent, right?"

"Blindfolded," he said wickedly.

"We'll need one for each wing of the floor that's able to gas up to twelve feet."

Shane glanced down at the paper in front of him. Michael, according to Chase, was notorious for creating extras in his poisons. He'd killed people in unimaginable ways, creating what he'd always called his masterpiece. He only hoped this time he would stick to just sleeping gas.

"Sara." Shane turned his attention away from the disturbing man. "You'll of course be waiting on the side of the adjacent building. This'll be our rendezvous point when we've retrieved the target. We'll need equipment, but nothing heavy this time. All we really need are ropes, screwdrivers, gas masks, and possibly a way to monitor security."

"Is this a joke?" Diggs sighed as he folded his arms across the table in front of him. "Why the hell are we pulling a child's playhouse job?"

"Trust me, Diggs," Shane said fearlessly. "It'll be worth it."

"We've done it before, many times. We can do it again," Trevor said.

"Haley." Shane practically whispered her name.

She suddenly felt all eyes on her. Sitting in the recliner with her feet underneath her, she gave a nervous smile. It was the first time in awhile she'd shown them any emotion whatsoever, and the shocked glances she received made her do it more.

Sara's eyes widened as she glanced from her to Shane. Her frown showed as she immediately knew they'd connected on a personal level. Jealousy hung over her like a black cloud ready to burst in storm.

"You'll be with me," Shane said in a soothing voice. "Trevor will go in through the side door, take out the security in the main room with the agent and then we'll head down to the vault in the basement." He looked at Trevor. "You'll proceed to the other two wings of the building to spread the agent and knock out the rest of security while we start on breaking into the vault."

"All of this for Amethyst?" Jordan asked, twisting his lips in concern.

Shane nodded. The disappointed glances he received made him realize nobody was taking this job seriously. With an eye on Chase, he motioned it was time to let them in on what was really going on.

"Amethyst is just a cover," Chase announced, standing up and taking over the discussion. "What we're really going after is something much more valuable." All eyes around the table gathered on him, and he proceeded without hesitation. "A small statue of an

Egyptian priestess was found during an archaeological dig outside Cairo about four months ago. Two black diamonds, a red ruby, and a string of jade are rumored to accent its black gold features. Story goes that this American who found it denied the museum its rights and brought the statue illegally into the U.S. Although this prize undeniably belongs to the Egyptian history, it's noted to be worth millions within the black market."

"So why keep this from us?" Jordan asked, intrigued. "Why not tell us to begin with?"

"This case is not from our upper management, if you catch my meaning." Chase looked at the puzzled group who stared back at him. "This is our ... personal operation, and one I am hoping will catch the attention of Yoshino."

"If this statue," Trevor said, concern mingling in his voice, "if it's really worth millions, don't you think there will be more security?"

"We'll have to take our chances."

By the way Shane and Chase looked at each other, Haley knew there was more to this story then what they were letting on. Finding herself slumping back into a depressive state, she left the now happy group and walked out onto the patio. With her thoughts on her order to kill Chase, she leaned against the stone banister.

Envisioning herself holding the gun to his head, she'd gaze into his solemn eyes just before she pulled the trigger. The heartbreak she'd feel afterward would be too hard to accept, and then she'd turn the gun on herself. She couldn't possibly figure any other way of dealing with the regret.

"Haley," Shane said, startling her from her desperate thoughts. "What's on your mind?"

"It's a good plan," she said, turning to face him.

"Thanks," he replied accepting her compliment proudly. "I didn't want to keep secrets from them, but I was afraid they'd go over Chase and turn it down on grounds I'm still considered a rookie around here. Chase would be in big trouble then."

Haley nodded. "I imagine so."

"I told Chase I didn't want you going, but he insisted you should."

She lowered her brows. "I've never been asked to sit out an operation, no matter what the job. I take it as an insult."

"Sorry," he spoke with a soft apologetic voice. He leaned back against the banister and took her hands in his. "I guess I'm just an old fashioned kind of guy, trying to keep the damsel safe."

Her eyes softened, amused by his concern for her. "I'm not in distress, Shane."

"You seem to be. Sometimes I'll look at you and you're so far away from everyone else I'm afraid you won't come back. Tell me what bothers you."

"What bothers me is the fact people don't know when to quit asking questions," she said, pulling her hand away from his grasp.

"The wall you've built is enormous, Haley." He grabbed her hand again and pulled her against him, ignoring her angry eyes. "Can you tear it down for just one night? Put your trust in me."

"I don't even know you."

Before she could stop him, he kissed her. She wanted to protest, but her body wouldn't let her as he pulled her into his arms, caressing the small of her back.

Telling herself to pull away, she lifted her arms and slid them around his neck. The kiss deepened, and like she'd fallen into a deep well, she lost herself completely.

Closing her eyes, she enjoyed the warmth of his tongue. He tasted sweet, chocolate mousse from dessert, and brandy from the drink he'd carried out onto the patio with him.

Intoxicated by his touch, the luscious and sensual kiss made her swoon. But it was suddenly taken from her when Chase walked outside to join them.

"Please," Chase said, "forgive me for interrupting." He eyed Haley. "I must speak with Shane for a moment."

Still light on her feet, she nodded and went inside. Trevor sat at the table alone, still studying the map.

She sat down in the chair next to him and watched him as he made marks with a red pen. His face looked serious, his typical expression.

"Why don't you take a break?" she asked, taking the red marker from his hand.

He glanced at her smugly. His jade eyes glistened from the light of the chandelier, but they didn't show any emotion. She hated not being able to read his body language, but she figured it was what made him such a good soldier.

"This job just doesn't feel right," he confessed in a low voice. He briefly glanced at Chase and Shane still talking rather seriously on the patio. "It's just too easy, too detailed. And I've never heard of this so-called priceless statue before."

"What are you saying?" Haley asked, intrigued by his concern. "Do you think it's a lie?"

"Something this valuable wouldn't have such minimal security." He lowered his voice to a strenuous whisper. "Nobody would be fool enough to leave it unguarded like this."

Haley thought for a moment. Regardless of the mistrust she had for Shane, she trusted Chase completely.

"I'll talk to Chase," Haley said, touching Trevor lightly on his arm. "I'll know if he's covering for something else."

Trevor nodded, pretending nothing was wrong as both Chase and Shane walked back into the room. He pulled the pen from Haley's hand and turned his attention back to the plan, continuing his marks.

Chase took Haley gently by the arm and led her away from the table. "Come with me so we can talk."

She saw desperation in Shane's eyes, obviously unhappy about something as he watched Chase lead her into the next room. What was going on between them?

Chase walked behind the counter and retrieved a small long-stemmed crystal glass. He uncapped a bottle of brandy and poured himself a shot. And when he downed it quickly, he closed his eyes. He let out a surrendering sigh, but didn't speak.

"Chase." Haley gathered his attention. His blue eyes were solemn when he looked at her. "What's wrong?"

"Haley," he answered in a soft, surprisingly unsure voice, one she'd never heard before. "I've come to love you like a daughter. It makes me happy to see you come out of your shell and show emotion again. He cares about you. Do you remember when I first introduced you into my house? You were such a pitiful young girl—abandoned with nobody on your side. I pulled you off the streets away from such filth and made you into a fine woman, a beautiful woman and a lethal soldier."

He fixed his eyes on her, but she turned away from him. She'd never seen him look so defeated. His mood was completely off, demoralized as if he knew exactly what she was supposed to do to him.

"When the time comes," he breathed deeply, "don't hesitate."

Haley snapped her eyes to his. Was he telling her this ridiculous assassination was okay? He couldn't know about it. And though she'd love to tell him so he could run, she knew he wouldn't.

"I promise," he said winking at her, "it will be alright. Everything will work out the way it was meant to, for me and for you."

He poured another shot of brandy and lifted the glass to eye level, inspecting it. His confident smirk returned as someone walked into the room.

"Ah." Richard's voice made her shiver. "It's lovely to see you again, my dear."

She turned around as he came to stand before her. She despised him more than usual, if that was possible. It wouldn't take much effort to break his neck right here, now.

"Richard," Chase said, greeting him sternly. "To what do we owe this surprise visit?"

"I came to hear about this job your crew is working on. I hear it's somewhat—perfect."

"It's a practice run to see how our new addition performs in the field. This is nothing but a trial—a small, simple coordination." Chase glanced coolly at Haley. "All new employees go through the same assessment."

"Yes, but what of the reward?" Richard asked curiously.

"Amethyst."

"Ah, lovely and somewhat valuable." Richard threw him a prying stare. "But tell me about the statue?"

Chase glared at Richard but offered no surprise in his face. He nodded for Haley to leave the room, and as she obeyed, her thoughts ran wild. How did Richard know about the statue? A traitor amongst the team was unthinkable, but someone had given him the information.

She gave Shane a horrified glance, trying to fight nausea forming in her stomach. She shook her head, refusing to believe he was the one.

"You look like you need some air," he said quickly grasping her hand. Without a fight, he pulled her upstairs and down the long hall to her door. He guided her through the dark space of her room and out onto the private patio. Stunned, she allowed him to sit her down on the chair.

He crouched before her. His striking eyes, darkened by the night, intently searched her bewildered face.

"Talk to me," he said. "What are they making you do?"

"Shane." She shook her head. "Please, don't."

"Don't what?" he asked sternly, taking her hands in his.

"You're working for Richard, aren't you?" she asked. "How else would he know about the statue?"

"I am not working for that ignorant bastard."

"Then how?"

"I don't know," he replied.

"Just go away. Get out of my room. I need to be alone," she said holding her face in her hands.

"You want me to go away when you need me the most?" he asked as he lowered her hands from her face. "I know they want you to do something terrible, something you don't want to do. Stop trying to deal with this on your own."

Shane was right here ready to listen, but could she really trust him enough to tell him this? Her mind was telling her no, but her heart—the way he searched her face, caringly, protectively, suspiciously.

She forced her confusion to the back of her mind and pulled her hands away, glaring profusely. "Why are you so eager to get close to me? Did Richard send you?" She shoved her way past him and hurried through the room to the door, eager to get away. But before she could grip the door handle, he seized her arm and swung her forcefully back around.

"Tell me what Richard ordered you to do," he demanded, pushing her up against the door. He held her face rigid between his fingers, forcing her to look at him.

The strength of his demand shocked her, and her eyes widened over the sudden severity in his face. She hadn't expected him to be rough, not after being so gentle before.

She fixed her glaring eyes on him. "I don't know what you mean," she said between clenched teeth.

"The truth, Haley! What are your orders?" he asked angrily shoving her head back against the door.

The pain instantly jostled more angry thoughts. Never before had she let anyone touch her forcefully, not like this. Though his hand braced hard against her neck, and his fingers held her rigidly under her chin, she could easily break free and turn the tables in her favor. But for some cockamamie reason, she couldn't find the strength to move.

"Tell me," he said in a low voice, his jaw tight, his eyes demanding.

It was then she could see the answer she desperately wanted. She saw pain behind his angry eyes—the fear and desperation of what she would confess. It was then she realized that he already knew her objective.

"Let me go," she breathed out her demand. It wasn't a troubling sigh, but one of defeat.

Shane slowly eased his grip on her face, but didn't let go. He gently ran his fingers across her cheek and leaned in close. And before she could protest, he pressed his lips against her temple.

"I'm sorry," he whispered an apology. "I didn't mean to hurt you."

"You didn't," she said, denying the enjoyment of his warm breath on her skin. A release of endorphins spread through her as he ran his rough cheek along the line of her jaw.

"I need to hear you say it," he whispered in her ear, working the warmth through her again. "I swear your secret is safe with me."

He moved his lips slowly across her cheek, and then pressed them delicately to hers. Surprised by his forwardness, her first reaction was to decline, but her head spun in acceptance.

Maybe the unclear thoughts of confessing made her return the affection. Like an open wound, she needed to heal and he was becoming her medicine. Normally cool and collected, she found herself anxiously pulling him across the room wanting more. And when he laid her back on the bed, she knew he felt the same.

He climbed on top of her, exhausting her breath with his mouth. The tension in her body flowed as he pulled the straps of her black dress over her shoulders, down her arms, and then coolly down around her waist.

Stopping to get a good look at her exposed body, he rose up and quickly took off his shirt. His perfect muscles tensed when she touched them, but when he pushed against her, a knock came to her door.

Haley immediately shoved him to the side and hopped out of

the bed. Sliding her arms back inside the straps of her dress, she gave Shane a perturbed glance. He quietly grabbed his shirt off the floor and went inside the master bathroom to hide just in time for Richard to walk in, without an invitation.

"Richard." Haley frowned, lowering her brows and wishing she'd locked the door. But the out of breath huff she gave was from regret for what she'd almost done with Shane.

"I apologize for my intrusion," Richard said as he walked right in. He glanced around the room as if looking for someone that shouldn't be there. "But I think you need a reminder of your deadline, young lady."

Haley swallowed the immediate illness she felt in her stomach. She stood rigid with her lips pursed tightly together as Richard examined her closely.

"Don't fret my dear. Once it's done, you'll take over this magnificent house. You'll have money to do as you please." He looked her up and down, puckering his nose slightly. "Go buy yourself a decent dress. You shouldn't look so..." his voice trailed as his eyes caught the curves of her body. "Trite."

His dirty grin grew as if mentally undressing her. He quickly reached out his hand, wanting to touch, but he only lightly traced the thin strap across her shoulder with his rugged finger.

He cleared his throat and stepped back. "Your promotion is in the works as we speak. I'm sure you'll have no dispute over your position once you see the cash overflowing your purse."

He reached out once more and touched her cheek with the back of his hand. Her eyes grew wide as he slowly leaned toward her threatening a kiss. Knowing she couldn't deny the filthy bastard what he wanted, she closed her eyes and held her breath, waiting for his disgusting old lips to touch hers. To her relief, he kissed her lightly just below the eye, and then pulled away. She stood rigid, staring forward as he walked to the door.

"I'll be waiting for your call," he said before he stepped out of the room. And as he closed the door, she heard him murmur the same line that had, since she'd been given the order, endlessly played in her mind. "You know what happens to those who betray the organization."

As soon as she heard the door close, she blinked. She calmly walked over and locked it, leaning against it to catch her uneven breath. The strong-willed woman she always presented suddenly dissolved into the frightened girl she despised. Her heart pounded in her ears as she desperately fought for control.

She couldn't show her tears, she wouldn't. Not by fear, and definitely not over something she knew was inevitable. There was no sense in dwelling on emotion. Regardless of the strong connection she had here in this house with the only man she'd ever loved, the only man that had ever shown her any shred of kindness or respect. She knew what had to be done. Chase had to die.

Her heart slowed to a steady beat, low enough to hear Shane's footsteps tread across the room. He drew closer, making his way toward her, but she refused to turn away from the door.

She felt his hand gently grasp her shoulder. The frightened girl needed to be alone, to sort out her emotions, but she let him turn her around. He didn't say a word, but his silence pleaded for her to say something.

"I don't know what to do," she said, her voice as steady as her averted stare. "I'm not a coward, but I …" her voice wavered into a soft whisper as he curled his finger under her chin and lifted gently.

He hoped to catch her eyes, but she refused to look at him. "I know how you feel," he said, offering a sympathetic voice.

She shook her head, startled by his choice of words. "You can't begin to understand how I feel."

"I understand more than you think I do," he replied.

"You need to leave. If they find out you know about this … "

"I'm not leaving yet," he interrupted as he grabbed her arm, a gentle persuasive hold, but she easily slid from his grasp.

"I shouldn't have got you involved. You shouldn't be here, Shane!"

"I'm already involved, Haley," he replied, his stern voice smooth and controlled. She tried to walk away, but he grabbed her wrists and pulled her hard against him. "Listen to me!"

"Why should I?"

His sudden angry eyes stared into hers with a yearning she couldn't figure out, but they softened as if he were withdrawing in defeat. He sighed, but didn't let go of her wrists as he spoke.

"Chase knew about the order when it was given. It's why he brought me here. He hired me to get close to you, to find out your intentions. I was supposed to persuade you to go away with me while someone else took your place." He turned his head slightly. "Of course, that didn't work out as well as I'd wanted," he mumbled incoherently.

She stood ultimately stunned, though she already suspected Chase knew. But to think he brought in someone from the outside to spy on her was unfathomable.

"So you lied to me?" she breathed her question, so soft she was sure he wouldn't hear it, but he did.

"I had to. It was the only way to get close to you."

She struggled to free her arms and succeeded as anger worked into her voice. "So all of this, it was just a charade to find out if I could complete my job?"

"No," he replied in a tone much deeper and calmer than it should be. "At first he wanted to know how difficult it would be for you to pull the trigger. It was never a question of loyalty. Chase knows your strong sense of commitment to the organization. But he also wanted to be sure of your struggle before he let you off the hook."

"Let me off the hook? I don't understand," she said, trying to control her rapid breath.

"He knows you'll pull the trigger but he's also aware of the heartache it'd leave you. He doesn't want you suffering with that guilt. That's why he wants me to take you out of the picture, so someone else can do it. You'll still get your promotion without a guilty conscience."

"That is the most absurd thing I've ever heard!" she yelled, unable to control her trembling voice. She turned to the door, ready to go blast profanities at Chase for being such an arrogant fool, but Shane stopped her before she could leave the room.

He turned her around and gazed at her, seriousness playing in his eyes. It frightened her, again bringing out the girl she despised as she struggled to suppress her emotions.

"You're not at all what I was expecting, Haley." He sighed, emphasizing his next words. "Everything's changed now."

"And what exactly were you expecting?" she retorted. "You thought I was some insensitive, unfeeling shrew that gets off on killing people she cares about?"

"Well," he replied. "Yeah, sort of, but now I know how soft and sensitive you are. And whether you believe it or not, you have feelings for me. Don't deny it."

"It doesn't matter how I feel," she said. "I know what I'm supposed to do."

"I can't allow you to kill Chase. Those are my orders, Haley."

"You can't stop me."

He hesitated to catch a breath, and then let it out. "It's true. I may not be able to stop you." He thought for a moment. "So then maybe you're right. You should go ahead and do as you're told."

An awkward silence passed as she stared at him blankly. It felt like an eternity went by as she held her breath trying to decipher his bizarre turnaround.

"What do you mean?"

"I'm telling you, as soon as you have the chance, take out your gun and shoot him in the heart, just as you were ordered to do."

She lowered her head, looking down at the floor, suddenly disgusted with him. "I don't understand."

"All you have to do is trust me."

There was something calm and honest about his eyes at the moment he left her arms. And as he walked to the door, she suddenly wished he wouldn't leave her there alone.

"Wait," she called to him as he stepped out into the hall. "Where are you going?"

He turned to face her. And at first she thought he'd come back inside and talk more, but he stayed in the doorway.

"I'll be back in the morning. I promise."

She watched him turn around to leave and a sick feeling suddenly crept up inside her. Suddenly regretting she'd said anything, she went to the bed, slid her fingers under her pillow and touched her gun for reassurance.

Chapter 5

"The malevolent spirit sleeps in silence until awoken by arrogant men," Michael whispered as Haley watched him work in the attic. "Righteousness dressed in black, stars on chests, dark swords drawn—unsuspecting warriors. Toss hell down a walkway littered with insolence, they exhale normally, but ..." He glanced up at her as he dropped the pin into a grenade now loaded with his sleeping agent.

"They inhale their last breath," she finished his bizarre story, uncertain whether to take it in a literal sense or not.

Michael grinned at her as he set down the grenade carefully. The gleam in his eye told her he was finally finished with his work, another masterpiece, she was sure.

"Breathing is overrated," he said with a chuckle. "We all eventually stop."

Haley didn't feel like listening to his crazy ranting today, but she'd found she needed to get out of her room. As she watched him load the grenades onto the loop of the belt Trevor was going to wear, she wondered why Shane hadn't come back yet.

It was almost one in the afternoon. He told her he'd be back this morning, and she'd waited for him in her room for as long as she could.

Every time she thought about Chase, firing the gun at his chest, vivid images of taking her own life popped into her mind. She wished there was another solution, but there just wasn't any other option. Better to die than live with this kind of regret.

"Michael!" Jordan's loud voice suddenly startled her as he walked into the room.

The grenade dropped from Michael's hand and landed with a loud clang on the hard wood floor. He held his breath as he watched it roll to Jordan's feet and come to a sudden halt.

Haley's eyes grew wide as she watched Michael rise from his chair and warily walk to Jordan. With a glare, he bent down and carefully picked up the grenade.

"Don't ever do that again," he hissed through his teeth as he stood back up and stared Jordan in the eye. "If I hadn't stuck the pin in just a few seconds before your swan-like fat ass walked into the room, we'd all be lying on the floor in la-la land. Can you imagine?" He chuckled cynically. "No, you wouldn't want to see Hell so soon."

The cool voice he carried surprised Haley. Although quite irritated, it seemed Michael would have been fascinated to find out what the agent felt like. He lived for danger, especially when it came to chemical warfare.

Jordan swallowed hard. For a moment he stood staring at Michael as he returned to his seat, but came back to his senses as he remembered what he came in the room for.

"Oh," he continued as if nothing ever happened. "I brought you the timers."

He held a small slender device with thin colorful wires intertwined inside and a curved metal hook on one end of it. The other end held a tiny, bright red button, and he used his free hand to push it in, setting it with a click. He placed it in the palm of his hand, and with a mischievous grin, stood watching it, occasionally glancing at Haley who also watched curiously.

"I set this little baby to go off in ten seconds," he said smiling proudly. "The red button activates the internal clock. And when it reaches the time, it sends the signal down through the wires into a spring, releasing the metal arm and," the device popped upward into a hook-like shape, "... wa-la. The pin is removed and the gas released."

"That's neat," Haley said.

"Neat?" Jordan looked at her closely. "Neat is a rich business man with perfectly groomed hair. This is a masterpiece."

"That's my line," Michael growled. "You don't get to use my line."

"I came up with it first," Jordan retorted.

"You did not. And you're not mad scientist enough to use it."

Haley left the room, leaving the two madmen to their argument.

She stepped down the spiral stairs leading into the large gourmet kitchen and breathed in the aroma.

Rack of lamb dressed with garlic and herb potatoes filled her senses. It would be a splendid dish at dinner—Chase's favorite. She dreaded thinking someone was making it for his last supper.

Where was Shane? And stranger still, where was Chase? He'd been gone all morning as well, which was unusual since he'd spent every morning in the library since she could remember.

As she made her way to her room, she did everything she could to think of something else, anything else, but it was impossible. Leaving town so someone else could take her place behind the gun was unthinkable.

She closed her bedroom door and sighed as she walked through the shadowed room toward the patio doors. Her heart began to pound, as if the sudden footsteps behind her fell in with its pace. The hairs on her arms stood as she tightened her body and breathed slow, ready to strike at whoever was following her. But when she heard his raspy, low tenor call her name, her entire body melted.

"Where have you been?" She quickly turned around and breathed an exasperated sigh when he swiftly embraced her. "You told me you'd be back this morning."

"I know," Shane replied as he gently pulled away.

His eyes looked as if he hadn't slept in days. And there was something different about the way he carried himself, a seriousness she'd never seen before. She shivered.

A knock on the door startled her. Shane usually hid from her nuisance guests, but this time he gestured for her to answer without disappearing, almost as if he expected this visitor.

She left his arms, her suspicious eyes watching him as he made his way to the bedroom window. He leaned against it, moving its soft see-through dressing to the side to gaze out at the plush green of the yard. Why was he acting so strange? She'd ask him once she got rid of this interrupting guest.

She opened the door and was surprised to find Chase standing there smiling. The sudden perplexity in his stare matched hers as he walked into the room carrying a gun in his hand.

"Chase?" Haley whispered as she saw the gun and silencer. She glanced up at him, wary of his intentions, until he raised the gun by the barrel.

He held it out, perfectly lined for her to grasp the trigger. Of course she refused, frowning as she folded her arms over her chest. She opened her mouth to decline such a foolish move, but she didn't get to speak.

"It's a gift," he interrupted with a heartbreaking grin. "I never really found much use for it myself, but I thought maybe you might...now."

"It's beautiful," she said sternly, gazing into his ready eyes. Had he practiced this speech?

"Take it," he demanded.

The look in his eyes—the same one he gave when he showed authority—made her take the gun from his hand. She inspected the black metal in awe. It was a flawless weapon, never fired, and fit comfortably in her hand. But she quickly held it out to him, emphasizing for him to take it back.

"I won't do it," she stated heavily as she lowered the gun to her side. "I should have told you about this from the beginning. We could have run." She gazed into his eyes. "We still can."

"Haley." He calmly grabbed her shoulders and squeezed. "You know running isn't possible."

"I'm sorry," she whispered, lowering her head in a bow. "I don't know how to accept this order. I can't!"

He glanced down at her trembling hand. "There is no need for an apology, my dear. I realized just how terrible this organization is a little too late. There is no reason to prolong the inevitable."

"I can't..."

"You have to, Haley."

She glanced at Shane who'd kept his gaze out the window. He hadn't moved, as if this was the plan all along. Would he really stand there and let this happen?

Chase took her trembling hand and raised the gun, helping her take aim at his heart. "You've pierced me in so many ways, Love. It's only fitting to release the bullet here." He pressed the end of the barrel against his heart beating like a fast drum. "Everything will be fine, but you must do as you're told. I would rather die a hundred deaths than let anything happen to you."

The tears welling in her eyes blinded her momentarily, but she blinked them away. Finally able to see, she was surprised to find extraordinary calm in Chase's demeanor. Any other man would beg for his life. And how odd it seemed he welcomed this as he fell to his knees.

Haley raised the gun, aiming at his chest. Her hand trembled slightly but she steadied it when she fingered the trigger. And then a strange calm worked over her.

"Remember," he said. "No matter what happens, I understand why you had to do this. I understand there is no other choice. Just remember how much I love you, Haley."

She closed her eyes and slowly squeezed the trigger. "I love you too, Chase."

She swore she didn't pull the trigger at all, but the sound of the bullet hitting his chest made her cringe, and the realism of what she'd done hit her hard. She opened her eyes and watched him, the man she loved dearly, fall over on the floor. Blood soiled his white button-up shirt and began forming a dark pool. And she knew then it was over.

The bedroom door suddenly opened and three men dressed in black rushed in. They quickly picked him up and carried his body out before she could say farewell. She wanted to call out to him, resuscitate him somehow, but there was no point of return at that range.

She quickly turned her tear-filled eyes to Shane, but he was gone. She was sure he'd left her alone to dwell in her own horrifying mistake. Remembering what she'd told him before, she realized she was wrong, completely wrong. She was indeed a coward, and taking Chase's life proved it. It was the easy way out. And now regret pained her heart, her mind, and her body as she fell limp to the floor and cried.

The image of turning the gun on herself crossed her mind again as she stared at it. It beckoned her to pick it up, and she listened. She pulled out the clip to see the number of bullets left, ready to use one more. But when she looked inside, she breathed a short confused gasp. The clip was empty, and the barrel was as clean as when he handed it to her.

Chapter 6

"Let me go with you," Shane insisted, watching Haley from the recliner in her room.

"You can't," she replied as she hung her black dress on the hook outside the bathroom door.

"The invitation was for you and a guest," he reminded her with a smirk.

It was true. The dinner party invitation at Mr. Yoshino's summer house on the other side of the city was for her and one guest. But this would be the first time she'd ever met him, and was terribly nervous to bring in someone new.

Since Chase's bizarre death, just a week before, she'd been contacted several times by Richard. He continually voiced how proud he was she'd stayed loyal and had done her job in a dignified manner, but she didn't see it that way. Dignified would have been turning the gun on Richard instead.

"I doubt you even own a tuxedo," she said as she made her way to the bathroom to take a shower.

Shane quickly stood and moved to the doorway before she disappeared inside. He eyed her closely, arching his brow. "I have one in my closet."

"If I show up with you on my arm, it might not go over well. It takes years to get invited to the boss's house."

"It shouldn't matter who you're with, as long as you're there."

"With the new guy?" she asked in a derisive manner. "I might as well be herding sheep through his dining room."

He chuckled, moving to the side to let her pass. "What if you showed up with your lover, and not the new guy?" he asked, gathering her attention abruptly.

She tried to figure out his intentions as he made his way toward her. His shadowed face was stern, serious, and quite startling to look at.

"If I were to follow reason," he said, coming to stand before her, "I'd turn away from you now and leave forever."

"Then go," she said, her heart quickening its pace.

"You see," he continued, grabbing her around the waist. He pulled her roughly against him. "I just can't seem to think straight when I'm around you. You are ..." He hesitated. "... dangerous."

She burst into a laugh, and her reaction took him by surprise, widening his mischievous gaze.

"You find it funny?" he asked curiously. Without warning, he quickly parted his mouth over hers. But when she refused his sensual kiss, holding her head like a statue, he slowly drew back. He ran his warm tongue across her bottom lip, gently, and delicately until he finally pulled away.

"Don't ever do that again," she said, doing her best to control her breath. "You need to get out of my room."

He shrugged and held his palms out as if he'd been caught stealing. "What did I do wrong?"

"Enough games," she said as she turned her back to him.

"But I wanted to kiss you," he replied with a raised brow, taking offense to her comment.

She opened the door to the shower stall, closed the door and undressed, using all her strength to fight the urge to pull him in with her. She started the shower and stood under the warm water, hoping he'd leave.

Through the fogged shower door, she watched him. She was sure he was catching his breath, and wishing she had pulled him along as his blurry form finally disappeared from view. She sighed in relief, thankful to be left alone with her miserable thoughts.

The image of Chase's last smile played in her mind as she showered. It happened every time she was alone. Every time she closed her eyes, even for a moment, he was there, staring at her. The understanding in his eyes—the love he carried for her didn't make any sense. How could anyone be so calm staring down the barrel of a gun? And though she saw him fall to the floor, she couldn't for the life of her remember pulling the trigger. She wouldn't have.

She turned off the water, pulled the towel off the bar, and stepped out. She buried her face in the warm cloth. It felt good against her skin as she made her way to the bed and sat down.

Her eyes wandered to the spot on the floor where Chase's blood had spilled. Over and over she'd relived that moment, and every time it still didn't add up. It just didn't seem right that he was gone, at least not by her hand.

She pushed her thoughts to the back of her mind. It was the only thing she could do as she pulled the dress off the hanger and laid it on the bed.

It had been a long time since she'd put any makeup on. Usually going natural, she decided it best to make her appearance a little darker for Mr. Yoshino. He was always presented as dark, mysterious, and ruthless in stories. He loved women, and they loved his money—and his power over an entire organization of misfit jewel thieves and unruly business associates.

Her heart leapt. She was finally meeting him, this man that stood over everything she'd come to know as her life, over everything she'd loved and lost. It was a little unnerving to be in the presence of a man so powerful nothing could stand in his way.

She picked up her black eye shadow and spread it thick over her eyes. Hiding behind darkness was the only way to go to this party alone. With one last glance in the mirror, she made her way to her dress. It was as black as her eyes, and it blended beautifully with what she carried in her heart.

She slipped it on. It fit snug, pulling her cleavage up along the top of the square neckline. Shortened slightly to above her knees, she knew she'd be attracting attention. Maybe this wasn't the dress to wear. She really didn't want any eyes on her, though she desperately wanted to impress her boss, or quite possibly she had someone else in mind, suddenly wishing he was going with her.

She grabbed her short leather jacket off the hanger on the inside of the closet and threw her arms inside the sleeves. She slipped her feet in leather high heeled boots that ran up to her knees and zipped them up.

With a long sigh, she opened the door to find Shane, dressed in a black tuxedo and waiting for her. He leaned back against the door with his hands in his pockets.

"Wow," he said. "You look wickedly elegant and stunning."

"What are you doing?" she asked, thinking he looked pretty damn good himself.

"I'm going to a party."

"No, you're not."

He stood up straight and offered her his arm, obviously not taking no for an answer.

"Fine," she said. "You're a persistent fool."

As they walked to the limousine in the driveway, she sighed. Though relieved she wasn't going alone to the party, the edginess wouldn't go away. She prayed Richard wouldn't cause a scene in front of the other guests, just as he'd done when he found out about her and Frank. She shuddered.

"I'm serious," Shane said, sitting down across from her in the limo.

"Serious about what?" she asked as the car pulled onto the highway.

"When I said you look beautiful, I meant every word."

"Flattery will get you nowhere."

"Just take the compliment and shut up."

"Oh, that's right." She flashed a sardonic grin. "You don't give out compliments often. So I should just spread my legs and let you take me here right now as your reward since that's really what you're working so damn hard for. Am I correct in my assumption?"

His jaw suddenly dropped open, but he composed himself with a clearing of his throat. She could tell he was fumbling for words.

"Do you have any idea what you do to me?" he asked as the car came to a stop at a red light.

"I have some idea," she replied, trying her best not to show him a genuine smile.

"No, Haley, I don't believe you do."

The rest of the ride was quiet; except for the few times he'd opened his mouth to say something, but only let out a short gasp. He desperately wanted to finish the conversation, but she could see how speechless he was so he remained silent.

When they reached their destination, Haley stepped out of the car and gazed at the magnificence of the home. Lit up like a small city, Yoshino's castle sat above the rest. It was an envious abode owned by a man who could make a criminal tremble and a saint bow down to his glorious presence—a true work of art she couldn't wait to meet.

Shane took Haley by the hand and led her up the steps to the front door where an elderly man, dressed in a white tuxedo and black bow tie stood watching them. His old eyes twitched slightly as he opened his mouth to speak.

"Good evening Mr. and Mrs.—?" he asked with a wave of his hand.

"Haley Branson and guest," Shane answered in a pleasant voice.

The man glanced down at his very short list of names. Finding hers at the top, he gave a slight nod. "Follow me."

"Thank you," Shane said as he pulled her with him inside the house.

"This is very formal," she whispered as the man led them down a white hall dressed in lovely red and gold accent.

"I had a feeling it would be," Shane whispered back as they passed an enormous staircase, reminding him of the one in Buckingham Palace.

Suddenly worrying she'd dressed inappropriately she began to fidget with the zipper on her jacket. Slowly zipping it slightly up and down, she followed Shane into the extravagant dining room.

A large eighteen seat dining table, fit for a king and his men, sat in the center of the room under a large crystal chandelier. She ogled, ignoring stares as she walked around the table behind Shane, who looked for their assigned seats.

He pulled out her chair and she sat without hesitation. She immediately caught the eyes of the woman sitting across from her. Dressed in a bright yellow dress and a dazzling smile, it was hard to ignore her. Large diamond earrings sparkled beneath her long honey hair that curled down past her petite shoulders.

"You're Haley, aren't you?" She spoke with a soft, high-pitched voice, as sweet as her friendly outlook. "It's nice to finally meet you," she said when Haley nodded. "My husband has told me so much about you I feel I've known you for years."

Haley didn't know what to think. She'd never met this woman in her life, and certainly didn't know who her husband was. Puzzlement must have shown in her face as the woman frowned slightly.

"Oh," she continued. "Please forgive me for not introducing myself properly. I'm Richard's wife, Gloria Boman."

In the years Haley had known Richard, she never would have

guessed he was married. Of course, it never really crossed her mind—especially to someone as beautiful and young as Gloria. The word cradle-robbing came to mind.

"It's nice to meet you too," Haley said, smiling graciously.

"Is this your husband?" Gloria asked, turning her glittering eyes on Shane.

She stared at him. An instant attraction, Haley was sure of it. Sara looked at him in the same manner, not that she blamed either one of them. He was quite stunning with those amazing eyes, dashing grin, and perfect body.

"Shane Sin," he answered before Haley could say anything. "And no," he added, being rather forward, "we're not married. We're business associates."

Gloria's eyes grew wide, mischievous indeed. "You two look like you could be a couple. Shane's aura is so light and cheerful, but Haley, yours is so dark. It's a perfect match."

Ignoring Gloria's pitiful comment, Haley's attention moved outside to the balcony. In the faint light of evening, a man stood alone overlooking the ocean. He leaned against the banister with a champagne glass in his hand watching the darkening scenery.

Seeing Shane terribly intrigued by Gloria's conversation about reading auras, Haley excused herself from the table and made her way outside. Warm air hit her skin as she came to stand beside the man who suddenly turned his attention on her.

His appearance sent her head spinning. She hadn't expected someone this beautiful to be here. His hair was as black as the night, and his eyes were a beautiful shade of deep blue that glowed in the dimming light of the sun.

He showed beautiful white teeth beneath his lips, and it was instant attraction, though not quite the same as when she looked at Shane. This gorgeous man was certainly dangerous. But when he ran his eyes over her body, she turned away. The attraction suddenly left on the gentle breeze.

He leaned his arm on the banister and gave her his full attention. "Excuse me for being so bold, but you are indeed the most beautiful woman I have ever seen."

Like she'd never heard this line before, though he'd spoken it like a true patron. His thick southern accent flowed beautifully, almost making her believe he truly meant what he'd said.

"What's your name, darling?" he asked, downing the rest of his champagne with a gleam in his eye.

"Haley," she answered, trying her best to turn her gaze to the calm ocean, but instead turned to look at Shane.

"Are you his dish?" he asked with a short laugh through his nose. "I recognize his face—the latest prodigy of Chase. The fool was always a sucker for big handsome men, which leaves me to wonder if he might've bat for the other team, so-to-speak."

Haley lowered her brows. "I'd mind my tongue on how you speak of him if I were you."

The man stood straight. He was tall, at least six foot three. He towered over her, but she stood unafraid and ready to defend Chase's honor.

He gazed down into her eyes. "I didn't mean to offend you. Accept my apology, if you will."

"We're here as Mr. Yoshino's guests. I doubt he'd be pleased to hear your shameful comments. And I'd appreciate it if you would address me by looking in my eyes rather than stare at my chest."

He chuckled in pure amusement. The urge to push him off the balcony was strong, but she refrained in the hope this party would hurry up and end.

"Again," he said, clearing his throat, "I apologize. I've never met anyone quite like you before. I like aggressive women. Maybe you should come upstairs with me later. I'd let you be as aggressive as you like." He leaned in close to her lips. "I'd pay you well for a night."

She immediately slapped him across the face. It took every bit of will power to hold her fist back as she left the rude man and went back into the dining room. She rejoined Shane and the other guests that had finally arrived. Luckily too many conversations were going on to take notice the deep scowl on her face.

A man in a white tuxedo came to stand at the head of the table. He cleared his throat, causing the room to go silent as he pulled out the end chair.

"Mr. Yoshino will join you now," he said in a rich proper voice that defined snooty butler.

All eyes scanned the room, waiting for the arrival of their host as Haley watched the man she'd slapped a few moments ago come in from the balcony. Her glare suddenly morphed into a fearful glance as he walked toward the table.

She watched him sit down in the empty chair and thank the butler for his assistance. A sick, dizzy feeling swept through her.

"Are you okay?" Shane whispered as she leaned heavily on the table.

Unable to answer, she shook her head. She felt his eyes on her and realized this was an impossible moment to get out of. If she left now, it was hard to tell what might happen. He'd have her killed before she left the front steps.

Somehow she found the strength to turn and look at him. Their eyes met, and his devious grin quickly became friendly. She managed to return his smile, but inside she was screaming, panicking, hyperventilating. She desperately needed air.

"Gloria, where is Richard?" he asked as he kept his eyes on Haley.

"He'll be along any moment, Mr. Yoshino," she answered nervously.

"You know to call me Devin. Mr. Yoshino was my father."

"Yes, of course. I'm sorry." Gloria blushed slightly with an obvious crush on him.

"Guests," he continued when he saw Richard enter the room. "I've called you all here for several reasons. Firstly, to introduce you to our new addition, our new gem who's taking a rewarding position in our company. And when I say gem, I mean a very rare and precious stone. I suggest everyone treat her with the highest respect."

Haley suddenly caught herself blushing, something she never did. The congratulatory nods she received didn't quite make her feel comfortable, but it did end her worry over raising her hand to her boss.

"The second reason I asked all of you here is to..." he paused briefly to stand. And then he raised his glass in a toast, causing a chain reaction of raised champagne glasses. "We're here to celebrate new directions. The changes we're making in my father's company are creating successful relationships with new clients, and even within our existing community. So here's to continuing change...and of course, making a lot more money."

As laughter rolled around the table, Haley could swear she saw a subtle hint of red in Devin's curious eyes. His last statement made her wonder exactly what kind of changes he was making, but it wasn't her place to question him.

"Anyway, please enjoy dinner." Devin sat down as a line of women dressed in white uniforms walked through the kitchen door, each holding a plate in their hands. They walked to the table and set a single plate down in front of each guest.

The aroma of roasted beef dressed in succulent vegetable sauce permeated the air as chatter suddenly broke out among the guests. Even Shane enjoyed the atmosphere as he began talking to another young woman beside him.

"You're a rather quiet one," Devin said, leaning close to Haley.

She didn't know what to say, still feeling rather conscious about her aggressive behavior. She set her fork down and offered him her attention.

"I'm sorry about earlier," she said in a timid voice. "I didn't mean to … "

"Bah," he interrupted with a chuckle. "My face might be red for awhile, but with good reason. There's nothing for you to apologize for when I'm the one who treated you rather disrespectfully. Accept my apology so we can move on. I'd really like to get to know you better."

He was quiet for a moment as he stared at her. She was impressed to see he kept his gaze on her eyes, rather than on other parts of her body. The blushing sensation wanted to return, but she held it back by redirecting her attention on her food.

"So what do you think of me now?" he asked curiously. "I mean is the bossman different than what you expected?" He rolled his eyes. "I can't believe I just used that term. Forgive me for being absolutely absurd."

She laughed. He was rather charming and quite handsome when he was being self-conscious. And though he was quite embarrassed over his question, she could tell he really wanted her to answer.

"I admit I wasn't expecting someone like you," she said, unable to comprehend why she began to feel quite comfortable with him. Maybe it was because she actually liked him, or possibly it was the buzz from the champagne.

"And what exactly were you expecting?"

She dabbed the corners of her mouth with her cloth napkin and placed it back in her lap. "I was expecting an older Asian man," she said, hoping it wouldn't offend him.

"Ah," he answered and nodded. "You imagined a strict business man, old and gray, barking out orders to everyone in the room. A woman looking at him the way you're looking at me now would be considered disrespectful." He shrugged as he placed his hand lightly on her arm. "That was my father. He was a ruthless Japanese man who won over my mother when I was a boy. I still can't figure how he'd captured her heart since I'd never seen him smile, not once."

"Oh," Haley said, arching her brows in surprise. "He was your stepfather."

Devin nodded, fixing his eyes on his glass of champagne, deep in thought. "I despised him. I've never told anyone that before, but I completely trust you."

"I'm honored I suppose."

He chuckled, releasing his hand from her arm. "It really isn't a secret though. Even he knew how much I loathed him, yet he still left me all of this. What can I say? For that I forgive him for every horrible thing he put my mother through. All the empty promises, all the affairs he had, but she still stood by him. Of course, I think she stayed because of me. He disciplined me and taught me everything he knew. I never liked the way he conducted business, instilling fear into the hearts of clients and associates alike. I swore once I took over that I'd never be like him." He sighed, leaning in close to her ear. "But I think everyone's still afraid of me."

Haley wasn't sure what to think. She wasn't exactly afraid of him per se, but she was afraid of asking him the one question on her mind. Why did they want Chase out of the picture?

As if he'd read her mind, Richard looked at her. He'd done it several times since he joined the party as if his evil glance told her to keep her mouth shut.

After dinner, dessert was served. A decadent chocolate mousse with whipped cream and fresh strawberries piled high in a crystal stemmed glass sat in front of her, beckoning her to eat it. She wondered if there was any other dessert recipe they knew, since they'd served the same dish at Chase's last dinner party. She excused herself from the table and made her way out onto the balcony.

The ocean roared in the darkness. A new moon left the view to her imagination. The daylight would bring her back with a surfboard to catch some waves, and it reminded her of the day she'd spent with Shane. And suddenly she found him standing beside her.

Shane looped his arm through hers and gently grasped her hand. "This is an amazing place," he said in a low voice.

She nodded in agreement. "I was just wishing it was light so I could see the ocean."

"It is a rather marvelous view," Devin said as he walked out to join them.

Haley quickly let go of Shane's grasp. She straightened her poise and pursed her lips, hoping Devin hadn't seen her reaction.

"You should come by sometime and I'll show you around the place."

"I'd love that," Haley said a little too excitedly, thankful he didn't take notice to it.

"My father bought this property for my mom as a wedding gift. It took five years for them to build this house and another year to build the private wing. It's far too big for me alone, so I keep it fresh with guests."

"This is one big bachelor pad," Shane said.

"I have to leave on business, so I'll get right to the point," Devin said coolly as he slipped into the space between Shane and Haley, separating them. He took her by the hand and gently kissed the back of her palm. "It was such a pleasure to finally meet you, my dear. I'm looking forward to our next meeting, which I hope will be very soon." His eyes sparkled. "As I'm sure Richard told you, Chase's house belongs to you now. The usual caterer will be visiting you soon. I trust you know how to manage it."

Haley nodded, but as Devin turned away, she stopped him. With her hand lightly on his arm, she pleaded heavily with her eyes. "Please tell me why Chase had to die."

He turned and glanced at Shane, and then back to her with a sigh. "I wondered when you'd ask." He gave her a solemn glance as he placed his hands on her arms. He squeezed gently, caressing softly before he answered. "I cared about Chase very much. He was a good friend and I miss him dearly. I have to tell you that it wasn't my order to give." He glanced inside at the tall gray haired man who stood smug as he listened to his wife talk.

"You know about the statue?"

He nodded.

"Did you know he was doing this for you? He wanted you to realize that your faith in Richard was a mistake. I should have—" her voice cracked as the tension got to her, but she would never become emotional, not in front of this powerful man.

Shane took Haley by the elbow, but she jerked away from his grasp, straightening her face. She gazed straight into Devin's shocked gaze, uncaring what the outcome of her little breakdown would be.

"Haley," Devin whispered. He leaned toward her and palmed her cheek. "I've heard nothing but wonderful things about you. You're loyal, smart, and absolutely beautiful. I see you moving up very quickly." He suddenly straightened his stance. "Both of you stick around for the night, if you like. There are plenty of rooms."

"Thank you," Haley said as she watched him walk back inside the dining area.

He joined Gloria, who stood alone near the arched doorway to the hall, and began talking to her. By the instant smile on her face, Haley could tell plain as day how much she was interested in him.

Richard was nowhere in sight. He'd probably gone off to handle more business, leaving his wife in the hands of her obvious secret lover as they both wandered off into another room.

"You want to stay the night?" Shane asked, placing his hands on her shoulders. He squeezed, massaging her with a gentle touch.

"I think I'd like to go home," she said moving away from him.

"What is the rest of the team going to think?"

Haley sighed. She too had been thinking about how they'd react. Sara wasn't going to be happy about it, but she figured she would be the only problem. She'd had a hard enough time staying on this mission without Chase—they all had.

"I guess we'll find out tomorrow," she answered.

A sudden image of Frank's death took precedence over her already horrifying thoughts. If anything did go wrong, she only hoped this time it would be on her and not on any of the others.

Chapter 7

"You had sex with him, didn't you?" Sara asked angrily. "I see the way you look at him."

Sara had pulled Haley away from the table after the meeting, lips pursed—most likely irritated Shane didn't want her. Not that Haley blamed her for reacting this way, but now wasn't the time to be jealous.

"No, Sara," Haley whispered. "Show a little class, will you?"

"Class?" She laughed cynically. "Don't talk to me about class. You're supposed to be this bad-ass woman, but you let Chase die! I just don't see how I can go through with this mission without him."

"You know there was nothing I could do."

"Bull!" Sara hissed through her teeth. "You're supposed to watch our backs. How am I supposed to trust you to watch mine now? How are we supposed to feel?"

"Sara ..."

"No, don't," she interrupted with a sigh. "I guess I shouldn't be surprised though. I mean, you let both Chase and Frank die, so I guess Shane will be your next victim."

Haley quickly slapped Sara across the face. "Do you ever think about anyone's feelings but your own? I never meant to lose anyone. I cared about Frank and I loved Chase more than you will ever know." She turned her eyes to Shane who conversed with Trevor and Jordan. "And I sure as hell am not going to lose anyone else I care about."

Her heart leapt to her throat when she said it. As she walked away from Sara's shaken glance, she realized just how deeply she cared about Shane, though love frightened her. She couldn't allow herself to fall for him—she wouldn't no matter how difficult he made it for her.

"Haley." Trevor motioned her over with a wave of his hand.

She came to stand between him and Shane at the head of the table, purposely keeping her eyes forward. If it was so easy for Sara to pick up on her emotions, then she'd have to bury them deeper.

"Are you okay?" Trevor asked, seeing the distance in her eyes.

"I'm fine," she replied sternly, refocusing. "What do you need?" He picked up a small leather black tool case from the table and handed it to her. "We've worked on this type of safe before, so it should only take a few minutes to crack and retrieve the statue easily. Once we've got it, we'll head out the same door and climb over the wall where Sara and Diggs are waiting. Then we're home free, I hope." He quickly glanced at Shane, a subtle hesitation of mistrust, but he quickly dispersed it.

Haley took the case and attached it to her belt and a horrible feeling suddenly rushed over her, making her shiver. Something was completely wrong. If Chase hadn't trusted Shane from the start, she would never have a part in this, and she was certain Trevor felt the same way.

"It's time to go," Shane said, glancing at his watch and then to Sara who stood in the doorway.

"The truck's ready to roll," she said.

Shane grabbed his black ski mask off the table and took Haley by the arm. He led her through the kitchen toward the side door of the garage, but then suddenly stopped. Sara and Trevor kept going, both giving Haley a perturbed eye as they disappeared inside the garage.

Shane quickly grabbed her around the waist and pulled her close. He leaned down and kissed her on the lips. It would have given her a rush if she wasn't so unsure about this heist.

He gazed into her eyes, but she only looked at him, brows arched, the shiver in her body passing through her once again. He would have to be stone not to feel it.

"You're worried about tonight," he guessed, a half-grin playing on his lips. "Don't worry, Haley. Everything will work out the way it's meant to. I'll be right beside you through this entire ordeal, I promise."

He palmed her cheek, but it offered only slight comfort. His hand was as warm as his light kiss on her lips.

"Why are you trembling?" he asked as he let his hand fall to his side. "Don't you trust me?"

She hesitated for a moment, dwelling on her thoughts as she gazed into his eyes. Maybe she was afraid to tell him the truth for fear he'd be angry with her, or maybe she was still just a coward. But when she nodded, it just didn't feel right.

He relaxed his eyes. The sorrow in them told her he had indeed picked up on her doubt. And though it bothered him, he didn't seem too upset.

"That's fine, Haley," he said, his tone much colder than before. "I understand why you're hesitant."

She watched him turn around and walk through the door. Her stomach suddenly turned in knots. She couldn't let him go after what he just said.

With a stride in her step, she left through the kitchen after him. In no time, she caught up and fell into pace beside him. As they walked through the enormous garage full of Chase's expensive sports cars to the long black Hummer waiting for them, she sighed.

She desperately wanted to apologize, but knew she couldn't. Even after they hopped inside the truck and sat across from each other, she couldn't bring herself to say anything.

Diggs and Jordan sat in back keeping track of the vehicle surroundings on the computer. Trevor and Sara were in the front talking about the escape route. With everyone distracted, she might be able to get in a few whispered words, but Shane beat her to the punch and leaned over, waving her closer.

His eyes were uncertain as he looked at her, lips pursed slightly. It was as if he were memorizing her face, every curve, every feature. And then he stared into her eyes with such seriousness, she felt they were alone. No chatter around them, no loud hum of the engine, and no tires rolling over rough pavement. Only the sound of her heart pounding in her ears made her aware of the way he looked at her.

"Whatever happens," he whispered in her ear, "I want you to remember how much I care about you, Haley. Don't ever forget that." He kissed her lightly just below the earlobe and then leaned back in the seat.

Her puzzled glance pierced his blank stare. He gazed over

her, watching the passing lights of the city through dark tinted windows. The slight twitch on the corner of his mouth was a good indication he was nervous, a normal reaction from a new recruit going out on his first job. His emotions were high, and she knew why he'd said what he had. It was the fear he'd get caught or quite possibly—killed. She'd never allow it. If anyone got caught, she'd stand right along with them. Same with dying, she'd stand beside him and take her well-deserved punishment.

She placed her hand over his, gathering his stare hoping it would comfort him. "I trust you," she whispered, and oddly believed it this time. It shocked her to say it aloud though it was just a whisper. She could tell it shocked him just as much from his agape mouth.

He looked terribly angry and shook his head in complete frustration. His hands clenched into tight fists, but he released them as he breathed out. And instead of looking at her, he turned his eyes to the front of the truck.

Haley wanted to scream at him. He'd made confessions to her. But now that she'd made hers he was going to shrug her off? She quickly leaned back against the side of the truck and let out an aggravated sigh. Maybe he didn't want her to trust him.

"We're here," Trevor announced as Sara began backing the truck into the alleyway beside the outer wall of the facility. "Synchronize watches. Once we're in, we have fifteen minutes after the gas to crack the safe and get the hell out of there."

"Let's go," Haley said positioning her earpiece in her ear.

"I'm in their network," Jordan called out. "Too easy."

Haley pulled the black mask over her head, attached the gas mask to her belt, and grabbed the rope. She got out of the truck, leaving her hurt feelings behind as she tossed the rope over the brick wall. The small three pronged hook at the end perfectly caught hold of the stone edge on the other side.

Trevor and Shane watched her from the ground as she began to climb, palming between each brick to keep herself steady until she reached the top. With her body flat against brick, she peered over at the small facility.

"No security outside," she whispered in the small microphone near her lips. "There's one inside at the front desk, two in the west wing, but I can't see how many in the east hall."

Shane and Trevor joined her on the flat of the brick. In unison, they removed the second rope from their belts, tied it to the hook and tossed the end over the other side. They shimmied down the wall and landed on the ground, immediately crouching to take cover.

"Going in," Trevor told Haley with a nod.

He put on his gas mask, and gave her a quick wink before he took off toward the building. She watched him as he took cover behind barrels and small crumbled walls, until he finally reached the side door.

She glanced down at her watch: two-fifteen. He only had two minutes until they went in after him. Her heart raced with excitement.

"I'm in," Trevor whispered. "There's three guards to the right of me—one at a desk, the other two standing in front of a door. Pin's pulled on the agent. It's live."

Michael was a magician. When Haley heard the thuds just seconds after the gas released, she knew they'd have the building in no time. She only hoped his agent wasn't altered to hurt anyone this time.

"I'm past the downward stairs to the vault. It looks clear, but dark." Trevor said. "I'm rolling another grenade, center stage view everyone."

Haley watched as the gas released in the front lobby. The man at the desk suddenly fell over. It was their cue to head to the vault— two minutes exactly.

"There's a guard heading your way Trevor," Jordan's voice chimed in. "He's leaving the eastern wing, holding a gun in front of him. I think he heard the commotion."

"Roger that," Trevor whispered.

As Haley followed Shane inside the building, she heard Trevor take the man out without a sound—the choke hold. Trevor was good.

"We're clear Haley, Shane. I'm releasing the last pin."

Haley followed Shane down the steps to the vault. He flipped a switch on the wall and the room lit up with a low grade fluorescent light.

"Here," he said as he made his way to the large safe nestled into a nook on the far wall.

Haley studied it carefully, recognizing it as one they'd worked before. "We need to drill," she said as she unzipped the bag and pulled out a hard shelled case. She opened it up and took out the quarter inch bit she needed and screwed it on.

Trevor came up behind them and took off his mask. "Wow," he said when he saw the combination lock safe. "It's an old model. I seriously didn't think anyone used these anymore."

Haley handed him the drill. She stepped back and let him begin his work. As he lined the drill up carefully, her eyes wandered around the room. It wasn't very large, and with dirty lime colored walls she could tell it was old—unused. Along each side of the small hallway were two long glass shelves covered in a thick layer of dust. It was then she figured out what troubled her most about this place.

"The shelves are empty, Trevor," she breathed out in caution, causing him to stop drilling. She scanned the entire room and caught a slight movement on the ceiling—a camera. Her eyes widened as a chill swept through her knowing that specific camera wasn't covered in the detail.

"What is it?" Trevor asked, knowing when Haley was like this, something was definitely wrong.

She walked back toward the stairs. In the corner of her eye, she watched the video camera slowly pan, following her move.

"Jordan," she whispered. "Are you panning the camera right now?"

"No, Haley, my eyes are on the safe," Jordan replied. "Why?"

"Where is the camera located?"

"It's hanging down in the middle of the room."

She turned around, her face pale. "The camera that's watching us now is near the entrance."

Haley slowly walked up the stairs, her skin crawling in horror. They were being watched by someone else. And just as she thought this might be a setup, she heard the sirens in the distance.

"Pack up!" she shouted to Trevor. "Blue is on the way!"

"Get out of there guys," Sara called out. "I'm watching them pass the alleyway now."

Haley motioned Trevor to go ahead as Shane grabbed her arm on the way up. He pulled her along with him as they made their way to the top of the steps.

Red and blue lights flashed outside and bodies moved toward the front door of the lobby, guns held high. Sirens screeched, causing the sound to echo eerily down the hallways of the building.

"Come on!" Trevor shouted, turning to wait on them.

"Just go!" Haley yelled, turning her head to make sure they weren't being followed.

They made their way out the side entrance. Trevor had already found his way across the small field and was climbing the rope.

"Get on the ground!" a voice behind her howled, extenuating his demand with a gun in his hand. "Get on the ground now!"

Haley desperately wanted to keep running, but someone wrestled her to the ground. She could've easily fought her way out, but Shane's hands were already cuffed behind his back and he was lying on the ground next to her. He peered at her, anger, sorrow, and worry in his eyes. It was useless to struggle now.

"Damn it!" He yelled as one of the officers shoved a knee into his back and pointed his gun at his head.

"Don't move!"

Haley dared any of them to touch her like that. She'd go down in a spray of gunfire if any of them tried. Luckily for them, her wrists were cuffed behind her.

They forced her up to her feet and read her rights. The Miranda Rights, the dreaded speech all criminals despised was recited to her in an angry manner. She'd never heard them spoken to her before, and a sense of defeat billowed through her.

She glanced back at the wall as they led her and Shane toward one of the police cars. Glad to see the ropes were gone, she was sure the others had gotten away—thankfully. At least they wouldn't have to suffer this humiliation.

She wondered how in the hell everything went bad when this was supposed to be an easy run. She'd probably go to prison for this, but again, maybe that's where she belonged. She'd be convicted of robbery, literally billions stolen by her hands. But no matter how much they interrogated or even tortured her, she'd never give up her comrades.

Maybe she'd even confess to murdering her beloved Chase. And her penance would be a jail cell right next to the man she'd fallen for, never to be able to touch him again. The thought made her want to cry, but she swallowed her emotions down as they shoved her inside the back of the squad car next to him. At least they were together.

"You okay?" he whispered.

She nodded, although it was obvious she wasn't by her frightened glance.

"I'm so sorry."

"It's not your fault," she replied. "We must've triggered a silent alarm."

"No ..."

"Shut up back there," one of the cops yelled, interrupting him and startling her.

He leaned over and touched his elbow to hers. He brought her some comfort, but the fact was they were heading to jail, and no matter how hard they could try, there was no way out of it.

Chapter 8

"Ms. Branson." A balding man in a bright blue long sleeve shirt walked into the interrogation room. "I'm detective Kaufman."

Haley sat at the table, hands cuffed behind her back, ankles shackled together. It was strange how they figured she'd be dangerous if she were free, though it was true. She could take down the entire police station if she wanted to. Hell, she could probably do it now if they hadn't cuffed her through a heavy metal chair.

He sat down on the other side of the table and stared at her. His thick brown brows lowered as he attempted an intimidating eye. She sat unaffected, blank, for it wasn't just his eyes watching her. Others watched her from the two-way mirror as well.

"No outstanding warrants, no previous criminal records, you're as clean as a whistle," he said in a pleasant voice. "So clue me in on why you chose a mix of thieves."

"I didn't choose."

He raised a brow, intrigued. "Are you telling me you were forced into it?"

"No." She shook her head, wishing he could just send her off to jail without all the questions. She hated being in the spotlight. Of course, if she just went ahead and confessed all her sins, then maybe they would stick her in a cell and leave her alone for the rest of her life.

"So you weren't forced? That would mean you did have a choice."

He clasped his hands on the table and tapped his thumbs together. She watched him, never looking him in the eye for fear he might see through her, putting her team in jeopardy.

"You mind if I call you Haley?" he asked rather nicely but didn't stop for an answer. "You know you're in a lot of trouble," he continued. "We've got you on breaking and entering, excessive force with intent to harm, an attempt to steal a priceless artifact, and possibly even murder."

"Murder?" she said immediately, without thinking how guilty she'd sound. She met his eyes. Was he talking about Chase? But there was no way he could know about that, unless…Shane had talked.

"Eight men are in the hospital right now. Whatever gas you and your partners used put them in a coma. Now," he continued politely, "if you're willing to cooperate by giving me names and addresses of the persons involved in your little heist, we could possibly work out a deal."

Haley couldn't help but laugh smugly. "I want to call my lawyer."

He sighed, shaking his head in disappointment. He stood up from the table and closed his eyes, just for a moment before he spoke again.

"Does the name Chase Elwin ring a bell?" he asked as he placed his palms against the table and leaned toward her.

Her smirk immediately turned into a frown. The tingling sensation of guilt poured over her body as Chase's last grin haunted her once again.

"Did you know his body was found a few days ago, shot up and dumped in a shallow grave in the park?"

The image of his lifeless body dropped carelessly was unimaginable. Whoever cleaned wanted his body to be found.

"What's wrong?" he asked as he took out a tissue from the box on the table. "It upsets you to hear about him?"

He brought the tissue up to her eyes, but she turned her head away, warning him with an angry glance to stay away.

"I think you better start talking." He tossed the tissue on the table. "I want names. I want info on all the heists you've pulled and any other information you have about the company you keep. Only then will we discuss a bargain."

"I have nothing to say."

He sat down and gave her a serious glance and then slammed his fist on the table. "The jewels you and your little gang steal are just a front to help fund his real operation. He's a drug dealer, a real chip off the old block, if you catch my drift."

She glanced at him blankly. This was the first she'd ever heard of drugs dealt within the organization. If there were any other criminal activities going on she would've known about it. It had to be a lie just to get her to talk.

"Come on, Ms. Branson, I'm giving you an out! Just give me one name to go on."

"Larson."

He wrote the name down on paper. "And who is this?"

"My lawyer," she demanded, fixing her perturbed eyes on his.

He sighed as he stood up. She followed his puzzled glance to the mirror, and a smirk escaped her lips. She imagined whoever was behind it was just as annoyed as he was.

He walked to the side of the room and leaned up against the wall waiting quietly. She wondered why he'd given up, until another man with rich dark hair and a cheap navy blue suit and tie walked into the room. The hateful look on his face was priceless.

Good cop, bad cop, she thought correctly as the man propped his foot up on the chair and leaned his elbow on his knee. He gave her an evil eye, but she wasn't about to back down.

"You'll go to prison when you're convicted," he said, his voice deep with spite. "You have no idea what terrible things go on. There's one place in particular where you'd rather die than stay in with the infestation of gang banger rapists and psychotic schizophrenics. I honestly don't believe you fit in with that crowd, so you'd best give us the info we need."

"I'm not saying a word until my lawyer gets here."

He lowered his foot to the floor and immediately threw his hand down on the table, causing a loud bang that reverberated through the room. His angry face turned beet red.

"Give me a name damn it!" he yelled loudly, and close enough to her face she could smell the sourness of his breath.

The door suddenly opened and Shane walked through followed by another man dressed in a police uniform. The cuffs had been taken off his wrists.

Haley watched him as he placed a hand on the man's shoulder and smiled. The man glanced at him, nodded, and then moved to the wall.

"I would have been here sooner, but I just came from booking," Shane said. "She doesn't know anything about it, Roger." He turned to the uniformed policeman and nodded. "Take off her cuffs."

It was immediate, the ill sensation in her stomach, nausea creeping up the back of her throat. She closed her eyes, holding it back as she tried her damnedest to forget seeing the badge at the end of Shane's gold necklace. When she felt the cop unlock the handcuffs and then the shackles from around her ankles, she looked again, and the truth spat in her face.

"You lied to me," she whispered, lowering her head to hide her heated eyes from him.

"Maybe so," he replied as he sat down on the table. "But it was for good reason."

She wasn't sure what he meant, nor did she care. As she pulled her hands up in front of her, massaging her sore wrists, she considered her escape.

"I see you're delving a plan in that pretty head of yours," Shane said as if reading her mind. "I advise against trying to escape, considering there are about fifty cops outside this room just waiting to take you down."

"Why?" she said through clenched teeth. "I trusted you."

"I'm just doing my job, Haley," he replied coolly.

She pursed her lips. "Was it your job to try to get me in bed?" she yelled. "How much did you lose on that bet?"

The other men in the room chuckled as he rose from the table. He leaned over it as she quickly stood up before him, causing everyone in the small interrogation room to draw their guns.

She sensed their anticipation, and she desperately wanted to test them. Maybe it was better to end her misery anyway.

"Sit down, Haley," Shane said in a deep growling voice.

"Not until I get an answer," she replied hatefully.

"Fine, I'll answer," he said calmly. "Sure, it might have been an incentive if you weren't so damned tight. I think Charlie lost fifty on that bet."

The realism of the situation suddenly hung over her head. He was indeed a cop and he'd set her up. The entire heist was a setup, and they all fell for it hard. How he'd fooled Chase into trusting him thoroughly was beyond anyone's guess.

Her eyes widened in horror realizing he'd be able to get her on Chase's murder. But he'd stood there and watched her do it—why... why did he let it happen?

The nauseous sensation came back as she fell back in the chair and lowered her head, hoping he wouldn't see the tears coming to her eyes.

"Give us a moment guys," he said as he walked toward the mirrored wall.

After everyone left the room, he reached up to the top of the mirror and found the switch. He turned it off so whoever was in the back room watching couldn't hear their conversation.

She watched from beneath her hair as he sat back down on the table and rested his elbow on his leg. His eyes were solemn, a completely different man than the overly cocky one he'd shown just moments before.

"Listen," he said. "Whether you believe it or not, I care about you."

"It doesn't matter how you feel."

"You know you don't mean that."

She gripped her hands into fists. One punch, just one and she'd feel a hundred times better. The jerk thought he could talk some sense into her, lie to her, or even speak to her now she knew the truth about him.

"You're a ... cop," she spoke through clenched teeth, wiping angry tears with rigid fingers.

He paused for a moment as he watched her. Curious, he reached out to touch her hair, but hesitated when he saw her wet hand.

"Look at me," he said softly, but when she refused he raised his voice. "Damn it, Haley, look at me!"

Haley shook her head, not wanting him, or anyone else, to see her like this. She'd never shed real tears for any reason in front of him, and she especially didn't want to now. He'd make her feel weak, humiliating her in front of his peers.

But then through the strands of hair, she saw him fall to his knees beside her. His fingers slid across her forehead, pushing the wet matte from her face. She raised her stinging eyes to his as another flood of tears rolled down her cheeks.

"You're crying," he whispered in fascination. He grabbed the tissue off the table and flashed a somber glance as he dabbed it gently across her cheek. "I'm sorry."

"Why do you care?" she asked, dangerously close to breaking out into a sob. "Just take your gun out and shoot me."

He blinked, surprised by her negative words. "Of all people, I'd never guessed you to be the suicidal type. Do you remember the day we went skydiving? I'd asked you if you had the chance to get out, would you take it. You could've lied, but you were brave enough to trust me. I'm giving you that chance, Haley."

"You don't need me anymore. Your foot is already in the door. You've seen everything you need to see to bust Devin."

"Sure," he concurred with a nod. "Maybe we could arrest him on suspicion of jewel theft, but he'd be out in less than an hour. His involvement overseas denies us jurisdiction to do anything more than slap him on the wrist and let him go. He has friends in high places at these auctions anyway, so it wouldn't matter what we tried to charge him with, he'd be protected."

"I don't understand." She shook her head, thoroughly confused. "Why go through the trouble of going undercover when you know that?" She let out a short gasp. "And how were you involved with Chase?"

He stared at her for a long moment before he cleared his throat. "Cooperate with me, with the police. Just tell me you'll work with me and I'll let you in on everything."

She couldn't bring herself to say anything. He couldn't answer her question, so why should she cooperate?

"Come on, Haley," he urged. "It's better than going to prison. Roger spent twenty-five years working in one. What he told you was no exaggeration. It's a vicious place for a beautiful woman like you, not that you couldn't handle yourself. But I'd rather see you free than locked up in a cold cell for the rest of your life."

She turned her eyes to the floor. Hopefully he'd realize she wasn't going to oblige. He couldn't make her betray the only thing she'd ever known in her life. It would be like turning on Chase and all he'd stood for. She'd rather die than betray him again.

The door to the room slowly opened, a fine creak of metal rubbing slightly together. With the awful noise and the thought Shane was leaving her alone in the room, she flinched. This would be her sentence, a lifetime of fending off her own criminal kind, and loneliness, terrible loneliness. It was exactly where she belonged— in misery.

"Haley." A familiar English accent disrupted her dreadful thoughts. It was the voice of an angel, the man she'd known most of her life. He'd saved her from the streets and brought her into his comfortable home to live, only to be irrefutably betrayed.

Afraid to look up to find it her imagination, she closed her eyes. She felt Shane's hand on her shoulder, squeezing gently, but she shook her head.

"I killed him, Shane," she whispered through clenched teeth. "I betrayed the only person I've ever loved, and now he's gone. I don't deserve another chance. I deserve to die."

"Now, I don't know about that, Love. I believe every life deserves more than just a second chance."

Did her ears deceive her this time? No—she'd definitely heard that rich, beautiful accent she loved more than anything. Her skin rose when she lifted her head and found him standing in the doorway. She trembled as if she were looking into the eyes of a ghost instead of precious heaven.

He opened his arms wide. And she did what any overjoyed woman would do—she ran to them. Undeniable guilt poured from her eyes. His touch was divine as he held her close, stroking her hair gently with the palm of his hand. And his voice telling her everything would be alright soothed her cries.

"I'm so sorry," she sobbed, pressing her face against his chest.

"I know, dear. All is forgiven, though there never was anything to forgive."

"I shot you in the chest, Chase," she reminded him.

"Ah, but you didn't. You were too deep in your emotions to pull the trigger, so Shane did it for you—a blank, of course. I wish I'd never made you believe this was the only life you were allowed to lead."

"I knew it," she whispered. "I should be angry at you for making me believe you've been dead all this time. But I'm just so happy to see you alive." It was the first time she'd genuinely smiled in weeks, and suddenly she carried hope for whatever was coming.

"Ah, my sweet Haley." He moved her back to look at her. "I am alive and well thanks to this man here." He pointed at Shane with a quick glance. A look of seriousness marked his face as he held her face in his hands. "The drug cartel exists, Haley. I kept quiet about it for a long while, but some...very unfortunate things happened. I couldn't let it go on any longer."

Haley leaned back on her heels and looked up into his eyes.

She'd seen this look before, a distressful gaze that usually sent everyone to their toes.

"What is it?" she asked as Chase pulled away from her, shaking his head in disappointment. She looked at Shane, pleading for answers.

Shane looked in the mirror and sighed as he flipped the sound on. He turned to face her, ignoring Chase's distress.

"We'd been tracking a local dealer for about two years now, hoping he'd lead us to his supplier. About five months ago, our undercover agents informed us of a big shipment of heroine coming in to a warehouse near the docks and their head honcho would be there to oversee distribution."

"Devin?" Haley said—not so much a question but more of a confirmation.

Shane nodded. "Of course, we've been trying to catch him on something substantial here in the U.S. for years, but we could never find anything to connect him to the drugs. We couldn't even manage a warrant to search the shipyard warehouses to find them until one of his alleged dealers agreed to help us. He agreed to testify as long as we put him in the witness protection program. So we finally got the warrant and rallied SWAT for the raid."

He sighed and glanced at Chase, then back to Haley. "When we went in, we found the warehouse mostly empty with the exception of the local dealer who hung from the rafters with a noose around his neck. A note was pinned to his shirt telling us the drugs were in a crate just below the body.

"Without thinking, a rookie cop hurriedly opened the doors. Instead of drugs, we found eight Spanish women with their hands tied behind their backs. They looked like they'd been beaten and dragged through the dirt, and they stunk like they hadn't bathed in months. Before we could stop him, the rookie untied one of the women, failing to notice the bomb strapped across her chest. The entire crate exploded, killing everyone inside, including six cops standing close."

"Were you there, too?" Haley whispered.

Shane turned and lifted his shirt and showed a scar swelled across the small of his back taking the shape of a slanted diamond. It blended into his skin so well, it was barely noticeable, but she imagined he felt it every day.

Chase looked at her and sighed. "I never wanted you involved, Haley. I wanted you out, not sinking further into this mess." He glared at Shane for a moment. "But it is necessary. Not only will your help provide you with a clean slate, but it'll tear down everything Devin Yoshino destroyed in his father's name. Takeo Yoshino was a good man. He's undoubtedly rolling in his grave over the new ruthless directions Devin has taken."

Haley nodded, feeling quite satisfied over Chase's words. It didn't matter if she believed it or not, she owed him more than her life if there was anything else to give.

"You want me to get close to Devin to find out where he's running his operation," she said without question.

"He likes you. But better yet, he trusts you completely," Shane said. "It'll be dangerous. But you're smart and beautiful, so it should be no problem for you to get close enough."

"How do you know they trust me?" she asked curiously. "Especially after this, I doubt they'd let me back in alive."

"It's taken care of," Shane replied. "We won't have any problems."

"We?" she asked.

"Remember, I was arrested too."

"No." She shook her head. "You can't go back."

"I have to, Haley," Shane said. "I'm already too involved. It'd look suspicious if I just suddenly dropped out of the picture."

She thought for a moment and then gave a short nod. "Then just tell me what to do."

"First we need to get our stories straight before we head back to the mansion."

A uniformed cop walked in the room, interrupting. He turned his gaze on Chase. "We're ready, Sir."

"I have to go now, Love," Chase said as Haley got up from her chair.

"Where are you going?" she asked, wondering if she'd ever see him again.

"I'll be safe. Once Devin is brought to trial, I'll be ready to testify against him." He grinned. "I love you very much, Haley. Remember that always."

He hugged her tight before stepping away. He followed the cop out of the room.

"We need to go too," Shane said as he gently grasped her arm and led her out.

She couldn't help feeling unsure of all this. She was never taught to cooperate with cops, leading her to believe Chase was seriously in over his head. And for him to agree to testify against Devin was unbelievable. There had to be something more going on, something they still weren't telling her.

She cautiously followed Shane out into the large lively room of cops, shouting over telephone rings and angry criminals. A group of them dressed in black SWAT uniforms walked into the room from the side entrance and headed toward the back. One by one, they passed them.

"They just got back from the raid at the mansion," Shane said, seeing the puzzled expression on her face. "It's probably a mess right now. Sorry about that."

But the stunned expression she held wasn't from the amount of policemen storming past her, but was the look for only one of them in particular. From a distance he looked familiar, tall, blond, bright blue eyes—terribly attractive. And as he neared, his face became irrefutably clear.

Haley stopped dead in her tracks, her mouth agape as the man walked past her without even a glance. She turned around, eyes wide in shock as she stared after him, intent to kill written on her bewildered face. She quickly tightened her mouth, her top teeth biting into her lower lip. She inhaled through flared nostrils and then said his name, loud and clear, catching his immediate attention.

"Frank?"

"Oh hell," Shane whispered, turning around quickly to catch her before she lost control, but it was too late.

Haley lifted her hand, clenched her fist and punched Frank in the jaw. The quick blow sent him stumbling back in shock. She wanted to hurt him in an excruciating way. To make him pay for the hell he put her through and the humiliation she felt now by his presence.

Shane grabbed her arms and held her back before she could continue punching him. She cursed, struggling to break free, but his hold was too strong.

"Haley," Frank said as he caught his balance, rubbing his jaw.

The surprise on his face grew into a condescending smirk. "I never thought I'd see you again."

"Calm down," Shane emphasized, trying desperately to control her outburst before the captain came out of his office and witnessed this. He'd surely have her detained.

Realizing Shane wasn't about to release her, especially with the group of armed men ready to step into the fight, she quit struggling. But when Shane relaxed his hold, she quickly jerked her arms out of his grasp and huffed.

"I can't believe this!" she yelled, massaging her throbbing and trembling fist.

"Come on, Haley," Frank said as if she should have known about him all along. "I had to get out. As soon as you and I ..." his voice trailed to a whisper. "You know, well I just got in way over my head."

"It took you an entire year to figure that out?" she asked hatefully. "I suppose I was just an incentive to you as well."

Not wanting to hear his answer, she pushed through a group of cops watching the fiasco. All this time she'd been grieving, feeling responsible for his death, but he'd been alive and well—a cop. She should be relieved to see he was alive, but all she wanted to do was crawl into a corner and cry—after killing him first.

"You're angry with me," he yelled after her. He glanced at Shane and then flashed a cocky smirk. "What till you get a feel of her."

Shane clenched his fist. He twisted his body around and planted it hard on Frank's nose. He heard it crack and then watched him fall back on the floor shouting out profanities. Shane leaned over him.

"You worthless piece of crap," he said through clenched teeth.

He glared at the stunned faces in the room and then went after Haley. He caught up to her at the entrance door, and took her by the arm, continuing their walk. She struggled with him as he led her out of the building and down the small flight of stairs to the sidewalk, but he held fast.

The sun was bright, causing her brief blindness. The tears in her eyes weren't helping a bit. She wished she had her sunglasses to hide her humiliation.

Shane quickly led her to the parking lot around the side of the building. He opened the passenger door to a dark blue muscle car, and helped her get in.

"What the hell is this?" she asked him when he joined her inside. She glanced around at the black vinyl interior while wiping away tears.

He turned the key and the engine roared to a start. It purred as it idled, and he cast a devilish grin. He was obviously in love with it and had clearly missed it in his absence.

"This is my second love—a 1968 Camaro Super Sport," he said as he put the car into gear. "I've been working on her since I was a teenager."

"Your second love?" she asked with a tired sigh. "So what's your first?"

He gave her a keen eye as if she was supposed to know the answer. "Well, you are, of course," he said as they sped out onto the highway. "I may have lied about a lot of things, but that part is the truth."

"Don't patronize me. It doesn't matter how either of us feels anymore."

She felt his eyes on her as she watched people playing on the beach. She wished she could go back to the way things were before she met any of them, back when it was just her and Chase. Life was much simpler then.

"Trevor would want out," she said, hating what this would do to him.

"I'm sure he would," Shane said. "It'd be too risky telling him. Right now, you and I need to get organized. We'll deal with the rest of them later."

"How did everything get so messed up?" she asked. "Devin just doesn't seem the type to be running drugs, or imprisoning foreigners to do his dirty work. It just doesn't seem right."

They came to a stop in front of a small white house with a chain link fence around it. The yard overgrown with weeds made it look abandoned. Haley watched him get out of the car and slam the door behind him.

He leaned down. "Are you coming?"

"Coming where?"

"This is my house."

She opened the car door and hesitantly stepped out. The place looked like a dump, scary as if it belonged in a horror movie. And its victim?—the unsuspecting rich girl forced to go in.

"Just come on." He motioned her to follow.

She walked around the front of the car, watching him as he made his way up the broken sidewalk to the small covered porch. He was happy to be home.

Chapter 9

It may have looked like a dump from the outside, but the interior of Shane's house was absolutely charming. It maybe needed a woman's touch, considering the large red neon beer sign on the wall above a black leather sectional couch, and a motorcycle parked in the dining room along the window. Various engine parts of a car sat on a small round dining table lined with an old dark green shower curtain.

"Want a beer?" he asked as she followed him into the quaint kitchen.

"No," she replied, trying not to show how amazed she was that the place was immaculately clean. "What are we doing here?"

As he pulled the refrigerator door open and grabbed a beer, he looked at her. It wasn't the same look he'd given her many times before, it was much different. The disguised arrogance was gone, and in place of it was a normal, completely relaxed man.

"I hate you," she said as she walked to the large walled window holding a view to one of the worst backyards she'd ever seen. It obviously hadn't been mowed in months, and car parts were scattered all over what could be an attractive patio area.

"You do not," he replied, pulling a swig off the bottle as he watched her sit down in the kitchen chair.

"If it wasn't for Chase, I would have killed you in the interrogation room," she said, hugging her knees.

"You're not a cop killer." He chuckled as he set his beer down on the counter. "But for whatever it's worth," he continued as he walked toward her, "I'm sorry for everything you've been through."

"I don't understand why Chase had to lie to me."

He stopped just before her with concern in his eyes. "You love him, don't you?"

She glanced up, finding his question curiously serious. "Chase is like a father to me. He's always been there when I needed him." She fidgeted nervously in her seat. "And look how I repaid his trust. I murdered him for what reason?"

Shane reached down and grabbed her hands. With a forceful yank, he lifted her to her feet and pulled her arms around his waist. And before she could stop him, he kissed her.

She shoved him back, freeing herself from his grasp. The angry glance she gave was not from spite, but from hurt, feeling again the humiliation she'd felt when confronting Frank.

"I won't be used again," she said as she started for the living room, heading to the front door.

"Where are you going?" he asked, following her closely. Realizing she was trying to leave, he blocked the door with his perfect body. "You can't leave."

"Get out of my way," she groaned. "I want to go home."

"You're in my custody. If you move a millimeter over twenty feet from me, you'll be considered a flight risk. Then I'll have to arrest you."

She leaned back on her heels and folded her arms over her chest. The way he smirked just made her angrier. "I don't want to be stuck here with you."

"Whether you like it or not, you are stuck with me, baby."

"Baby?" She clenched her teeth, trying her best to keep from losing her temper. This was going to end up in a huge fight.

"Cool your jets, Haley," he said, lowering his brows. "Just sit down and stop acting like a spoiled brat."

It was an immediate reaction, the palm over fist stance. She twisted her body, stretched her arm with a quick jerk, and planted her hand across his face.

The blow sent him stumbling back, obviously not expecting it, but he'd given her no choice. With his degrading words, he deserved to be put in his place to remember who he's dealing with.

He stared at her in awe with his hand touching his cheek. At first she thought maybe she'd gotten through to him, but when he scowled, she knew he was ready for a real fight.

"Well," he said shaking the pain off as he began walking around her. "I could draw my gun and shoot you for assaulting a police officer."

"You keep throwing the fact you're a cop in my face. Do you really think I care?"

"Why yes, I believe you've told me several times that you do." He chuckled, throwing in a quick light tap on her face as he began to dance around her like a boxer in a ring.

"Stop," she insisted. He'd caught her off-guard, but she wouldn't let it happen again.

He looked ridiculous, dancing around her in circles as if he were the boxer playing with his foe. It was distracting. And the way his friendly eyes watched her was making her anger subside.

"What's wrong?" he asked, still dancing along side her as she made her way back to the kitchen. He punched her lightly on the arm, the shoulder, the back. "I thought you wanted a fight."

His whine intensified and she finally beamed. She shook her head and rolled her eyes. He wasn't only being ridiculously charming, but cute as well.

She leaned back against the counter, meeting his eyes as he stopped before her with his silly grin. He caressed her face with his palm and gently brushed her hair back over her ear. The moment made her dizzy, but it wasn't from his sensual touch.

It seemed all the years of bottled pressure suddenly released. She fell to her knees and let the warm liquid stream down her face.

Her entire life had been a sham. Everything she'd ever known was nothing but a cover for an underlying evil. Chase, Frank, and now Shane had been the most important people in her life, and they had all deceived her. Had she really been that gullible, so vulnerable that she couldn't see who they truly were?

All the pain she'd caused, all the pain she'd endured suddenly came out in fits of tears. Coming unglued was Shane's fault, but she had no one else to blame for her mistakes but herself.

"I'm so sorry," she cried when she felt Shane's hands touch her shoulders. He lifted her to her feet and pulled her into his arms.

"What's wrong?" he asked, his playful voice suddenly changing into a soothing tenor. "Haley." He gently tucked his finger under her chin and lifted her eyes to his. "Talk to me."

She returned his gaze with swollen eyes unable to put on her usual front and bottle her emotions. "I killed everyone I've ever loved."

"Don't be silly." He chuckled as he pushed back a dark strand of her hair caught on her pouting lip. "Chase is very much alive. Frank, well, he's an ass, but he's alive too. And look at me." He grasped her hand and held it to his face. "I'm not dead, Sweetheart. I'm right here with you."

She pressed her cheek against his chest, and then closed her eyes.

"I understand how you're feeling," he said as he put his strong arms around her shoulders and held tight. "I'll do what I can to help you through this."

"I killed Chase," she whispered, reliving the memory.

"He may be stuck in a stuffy safe-house, but he's alive. You didn't pull the trigger, Haley. You couldn't hurt anyone."

She shook her head agitated at him for being too understanding. He was a cop for God's sake! And she didn't deserve his patronage.

"I put my gun to his heart. I meant to do it. It's inexcusable!"

"Haley," he argued. "They forced you ..."

"No!" she yelled angrily, clenching her teeth as she moved back away from him. "I had a choice. The gun was in my hand, and I would have done it. I would have killed him!"

He followed her until she was trapped against the wall. He squeezed her arms firmly in his hands and shook her, just enough to gather her attention. "You've been in this dirty organization far too long," he said. "If Chase didn't die, they would have killed you both." He sighed in frustration. "It set us in the right direction. So don't stand there feeling sorry for yourself. If you want to make amends, then clean yourself up and help with the damned investigation."

She wiped her face and thought something she'd never before thought in her life. "I'm scared." She looked down, embarrassed by her confession. "What if I'm too weak to refuse their next order?"

"You've been brainwashed," he retorted. "Chase agreed to help us on condition we get you out as well." He shook her gently to emphasize his words. "You will do everything you can to help us. If they ask you to do anything—and I mean anything you don't feel comfortable doing, let me know. I'll take care of you. I promise. Do you understand?"

She threw him a puzzled glance and then left his grasp. She walked to the window, wondering what part the innocent women in his story had. Who were they? And why didn't anyone protect them?

"What is it?" he asked as he leaned back against the wall, watching her intently.

"If Chase knew about this for so long, he hid it well. When did you two meet?"

He twisted his lips, momentarily thinking, or quite possibly hesitating to answer. But when he looked at her, he smiled as if he'd expected her to ask this.

"It's a funny story, actually," he said, recollecting his memory. "I met him about three years ago during a drug bust at one of the stores on the walkway."

Haley gasped. "Three years?"

Shane nodded. "Chase was shopping there when we took down the store owner and a few of his clients dealing in back. Of course, we didn't know he was innocent until we dragged him down to the station and questioned him. I was lead in the investigation, so I believed him when he said he had no idea what was going on. I was surprised when he invited me out for a beer afterward. Nice guy," he added with a grin.

"Anyway, about a year and a half ago, he contacted me in private. He told me about Yoshino and the new direction he was taking his father's business. Of course, we've been trying to get the bastard for awhile, so it was amazing to have this fall into our laps. Unfortunately, Chase was overseeing your group and wasn't supposed to know about the drugs. But we sent someone in anyway just to take a look around."

Haley had to sit down. She thought back to when all this would have happened, but all she could remember about that time was Frank.

She quickly looked up and found her answer written all over Shane's guilty face. "You sent Frank in, didn't you?"

He confirmed with a nod and then pursed his lips. "I'm really sorry. I had no idea he'd get himself involved like that." He sighed. "I should have pulled him out when I heard he was getting too close."

She caught sight of the odd look on his face when he cleared his throat. "You're jealous, aren't you?"

He shook his head, but his eyes gave him away. "If I knew then what I know now," he said with a perturbed growl, "I would never have picked him to play the part. He's an idiot for wanting out—for wanting to be away from you. I would have done anything to stick around."

"You don't mean that."

"Don't I?" he asked with a thrill in his voice. "Skydiving with you is a fantasy come true."

Haley frowned.

"We'll do it again," he promised. "Once this is over, I'll take you skydiving over the Grand Canyon. We'll land on one of the canyon trails and hike our way out, camping at night, exploring the caverns during the day. Can you imagine us tucked inside a sleeping bag, keeping each other warm?"

"Shut up," she said curtly. "I don't want to hear about your ridiculous little fantasies. They'll never come true."

"Why not?" he asked, almost sounding as if his feelings were hurt.

She stared him straight in the eye. "Because you're a cop, and I'm a criminal."

For a long moment everything grew silent. The only sound came from the ticking clock above the kitchen doorway. The sun suddenly faded, hiding behind gray clouds threatening rain. And then finally, Shane cleared his throat.

"Follow me," he said, reaching out to take her hand. Glad she accepted without a fuss, he pulled her down the hallway. "I really didn't want to show you this," he said as he led her into his bedroom. "But I think it's time you know."

A desk sat in the corner of his darkened room. Papers strung out around his computer. But as messy as it was, he knew exactly where to look as he pulled out a slightly tattered manila folder and sat down on the workstation chair.

Haley sat down on the bed across from him and watched intently as he opened the folder with sulking eyes. Returning his attention to her, he pulled out a photo and held it out.

"Recognize him?" he asked and then waited for her response.

Her eyes fell on the man in the photo as she took it from his hand. His face was all too familiar, and one representing her entire disgusting childhood. She suddenly lost her breath. The photo slipped from her fingers and fell to the floor.

"What now?" she asked in a gasping breath, trying desperately to keep her sanity.

Shane sighed as he bent over and retrieved the photo from the floor. "You do recognize him, don't you?"

She nodded, somehow controlling her trembling lips.

"He was the dealer we found strung from the rafters."

"He got what he deserved," she said, her serious voice threatening a condescending laugh.

"Chase said this was the guy he took you from. He said most of the dealers use women to deliver their product and you were one of the unfortunate. Most of the women are foreign, taken from poverty. They're desperate. They'll do whatever's asked of them. It leads me to wonder how you got involved."

"What do you want me to say?" she asked with a sturdy voice.

He rose from his chair and sat down beside her on the bed. He slid his palms over her face and stroked her lips with his thumb, gazing into her eyes. "How could such a dark-haired, fair-skinned beauty end up here?" He leaned close and kissed her gently above the eye. "Where do you fit in?"

Before she could answer, he kissed her lips. It made her skin rise and excitement rushed through her. But she quickly pulled away as the memories from her past began to haunt her.

"What is it?"

"I'd like to shower and change." She glanced down at the black jumpsuit she still had on from the heist and frowned.

"Not going to answer me yet, huh?" he asked as he stood up. "The shower's across the hall. You can check my closet for something to wear."

"Thank you."

"Sure," he acknowledged, and then lifted a curious brow. "Are you as hungry as I am?"

She nodded as she began looking through his closet, his police uniforms catching her eye.

"I'll make us something," he said quietly and then left the room.

She pulled a dark blue police shirt off the bar. As she studied it, a chill crept over her. She never dreamed she'd ever work with the police. Yet here she was in the house of one who'd not only caught her thieving hand, but caught her heart as well.

She closed her eyes and breathed in the aroma. His scent was so masculine, so intoxicating. A frown tainted her lips as she hung the uniform back on the bar. She pulled a simple white shirt from a hanger and walked across the hall.

The bathroom was small, quaintly decorated in white and blue tile. With only room enough for a stand up shower, a small toilet, and a tiny walled sink, she could have entered the closet instead.

She began to undress, feeling the coldness of the floor on her feet. She sighed as she stripped off the jumpsuit. She tossed it on the floor, shivering as the air caught her bare skin. It felt wonderful.

She reached in and turned the shower on, but noticed there wasn't any soap. She opened the bathroom door and leaned out looking around for a linen closet.

"Shane," she called out and waited for a moment. Thinking maybe he'd gone outside, she left the confines of the bathroom and went to his room.

He was very much a bachelor. The bottle of cologne, shaving cream, and razor seemed part of the décor on his dark stained wood dresser. She knew it was wrong to be relieved he wasn't married. It really shouldn't matter since there could never be anything between them.

But curiosity got the better of her as she opened the top drawer, half expecting, and hoping, to find some hint he was involved with someone. She found his underwear, rolled perfectly and tucked with organization of color. Unable to fight the oncoming grin, she let it slip and then searched the drawer with her hand.

Just as she figured, she found something hard inside. She pulled the item out of its resting place and let out a short gasp.

A semi-automatic, holstered in a black leather glove, shined brilliantly in the dim light of the room. She unsheathed it and studied it carefully. This definitely wasn't standard issue for a cop. What was he doing with something so powerful? And more importantly, why was it dressed with a silencer?

She studied the weapon in fascination. It was beautiful, black metallic like the shine from a car. It was easy to grip. The scope was waxed, perfectly aligned as she stared down the line and fingered the trigger.

"I could stand here and watch this all day," his voice called from the doorway.

Startled, she stuffed the gun back inside the holster and then the drawer. She turned to face him, the guilty look on her face won over the shyness of being caught completely naked.

He walked to her, reached down, and then closed the drawer as if telling her in a nice way to stay out of it. Maybe he was.

"You don't have to ask," he said, eyeing her body with a look of intent. "It's my undercover weapon."

"I was only looking for soap," she said as she folded her arms across her chest.

"You were snooping." He chuckled. "There's soap in the linen closet, where most soap is normally kept."

He pushed a strand of her hair over her shoulder making her shiver slightly. He groped her body with his eyes and she thought for sure he was going to pull her into his arms, throw her onto the bed and make mad passionate love to her. But he frowned when he turned away heading to the bathroom.

She followed him, embarrassed, even a bit hurt he'd turned away so quickly. And as she watched him reach into the small closet behind the door and pull out a bar of soap, hurt turned to curiosity.

"What's wrong?" she asked him as he handed her the bar.

"What do you mean?" he replied as he pulled out a large white towel.

"You don't find me attractive?"

He gave out a short emphasized laugh. "Don't be ridiculous." He growled as he wrapped the towel around her.

"Then why are you looking the other way?"

"Believe me," he answered. "It's difficult to do when you're parading through my house naked." He frowned. "The truth is I don't want to take advantage of you while you're vulnerable. You've had a lot to chew on in the last twenty-four hours."

She watched him leave. Heat rushed to her face not only from being caught browsing in his room, but angry he'd called her vulnerable.

She clenched her teeth as she turned the shower on, but slowly the truth sunk in. He was right. She had no idea what she was going to do or what was going to happen. As tough as she was, her heart sank every time she thought about staying in the huge mansion alone wondering if anyone found out she'd began working for the cops. They'd kill her, and she'd never see it coming. Living in fear was something she wasn't prepared to do.

Right now, as much as she despised it, Shane was the only thing keeping her from losing her mind. She suddenly wanted to feel his arms around her—medicine for the vulnerability he'd accused her of.

As she let the warmth of the water run over her head she tried not to think. Washing the nightmare of the past two days away, even for just a brief moment, was all she wanted to do, but her thoughts went to the powerful gun in his drawer.

Why had he lied to her about it? There was no way an undercover agent carried such a weapon in the United States. But in another country like Mexico ... Her eyes widened at the thought—the same gun would be completely permissible.

Chapter 10

"This is all her fault!" Sara yelled, trying to break free from Diggs' grasp. She already lucked out on one slap across Haley's face, but she wanted more. "Just look around! Look at what the bastards did to Chase's house!"

Haley watched tears flow from Sara's eyes as she held her reddening cheek. On another day she would have quickly pinned her to the floor and inflicted pain on the young girl, but today she knew Sara deserved to lash out.

"They didn't find anything," Trevor said coolly as he glanced at the mess of papers and broken glass scattered across the floor. "So mind your tongue Sara. This isn't anyone's fault." He eyed Shane suspiciously. "I thought you had this all planned out. What the hell happened last night?"

"Someone tripped the silent alarm," Shane said as he leaned against the wall.

"There's no sense in putting blame on him either," Haley scowled. "I'm just glad everyone got away."

"And how did you manage to escape?" Trevor asked, arching his brow. "I saw both of you swarming in blue."

Shane moved his attention from Haley to Trevor. "She's a genuine Houdini when it comes to cuffs, but ingenious with locked doors."

Haley turned her eyes away from the disgruntled group. She hated lying to them, even with something as poor as Shane's excuse, but it seemed to work.

"Well," Trevor said with a quick sigh. "I guess we better clean up."

"Clean it your damned self!" Sara jerked away from Diggs' large hands and glared hatefully at Haley as she stormed out.

Haley watched as Diggs followed giving her his own unruly look before he disappeared through the doorway. She held her breath, unsure if she could take any more of this.

She let it out as she too stormed off, but in the other direction. With quickness to her step she found herself walking toward her room. She wanted to be alone, to shout in agony how much she hated all of this, but someone grabbed her arm and stopped her.

She immediately scowled, assuming it was Shane. "I need time alone," she emphasized her words as she was turned around. But when she caught deep blue eyes in hers, she gasped.

"Haley," Devin said with a grim smile.

She peered up into his eyes forgetting her place. He was handsome and way too friendly looking to be this horrible drug lord they'd warned her of. But when she thought of the women being used and killed as a warning, she gathered her senses.

"I apologize for my tone," she said in a calm voice. "What can I do for you?"

He grinned just as she'd seen him do at his party, so well-mannered, but this time she saw the devil in his eyes.

"So the job didn't go as planned," he said as he tucked her arm under his and walked her down the arched breezeway. Rather than look at her, he kept his gaze forward as he spoke.

Haley felt her heart pound in her chest. Two rather large, darkly dressed men—bodyguards, walked at a distance behind them, but she remained cool as she explained Shane's cockamamie story. She only hoped he believed her.

"We triggered a silent alarm. Shane and I were the only ones caught, but we managed to escape before they could identify us."

"I heard." He nodded as he led her through the patio door and let go of her arm.

He stuck his hands in the pockets of his dark slacks and leaned back against the stone banister. Green vines entwined around the large grey pillars holding up the enclosed porch.

"It was a mistake," she continued. "We'll learn from it and move on to our next …"

"There won't be a next," he blurted, interrupting her.

The way he held his eyes on her was strange, much different than the last time he stared. They wandered over her as if searching her soul, reading her mind, or possibly peeling her clothes off. It made her feel uncomfortable and she switched her weight to the other foot.

"What do you mean?" she asked feeling the nervous strain in her throat.

He turned away and gazed out across the green grass of the yard. Happy his eyes had left her, she walked in beside him and leaned against the banister. It was time to start her act.

She could tell he enjoyed her touch as she brushed her arm against his causing him to face her yet again. His glance lingered on her, brushing her cheek, her lips, her eyes.

"Your team's being disassembled, and this mansion sold. You're much too good for this kind of work anyway. What I'd like is for you to come live in my house on the coast."

Her mouth opened in shock, but she quickly tightened her lips in a straight line. "I like it here," she said in earnest.

"I understand your sentiment," he replied with a nod. "I'm sure this house holds great memories for you. But that's all this is, Beautiful, just a house. There are no connections here anymore. No warm bodies or friendly faces to keep you company with conversation. There are only ghosts here."

He glanced at his two bodyguards and motioned with a nod for them to leave. Without a word or gesture, they disappeared from the doorway.

He brought his hand to her face and touched her cheek lightly with his palm. With a gentle glide, he pushed his strong fingers through her fine black hair.

"You are, you know." he whispered as he found her cheek again.

"What?" she asked softly, trying not to show how much she despised his touch.

"You're the most beautiful woman I've ever seen. And I will be honest—there are ulterior motives to my invitation, besides a job, if you will."

He slid his fingers back and grasped her head in his hand. He pulled her slowly toward him, desiring a kiss. And though it irrefutably annoyed her, she would allow it for the cause.

His lips were soft, the kiss gentle. Never advancing his tongue, he pressed his lips to hers, pulling tenderly. She closed her eyes, letting his other hand touch the other side of her face until both hands held her to him.

Closing her eyes, she envisioned Shane, causing the kiss to deepen. His strong hands slowly moved down her neck, over her shoulders, and then to her arms. They caressed her hips and made their way around her waist. A smile crept across her lips, indulging in him for just a little while, at least until she opened her eyes.

Deep ocean blue sparkled at her, bringing her back to reality. She quickly pulled away from his embrace, half-heartedly smiling.

"I'm sorry," she apologized.

"For what?" he asked. "That was remarkable." He reached for her again, but she backed away, just enough to make him believe it was a playful tease.

"You never told me what kind of job you were offering."

"Oh, yes, the job," he said with a nervous clearing of his throat, his head still swimming in delight. "I want you to be my assistant."

"Assistant?" she asked.

"Yes," he replied. "You'll help me stay on schedule. Since my last assistant left, I've had such a difficult time keeping up with everything. Shipments are coming in on the docks, dinner parties, and trips overseas. I just can't find time to schedule in a breath." He chuckled with a shimmer in his eye. "I realize it's a far cry from your current, though I'm sure rather exhilarating job, but I can't think of a better candidate."

"What about Richard's wife?"

He stood for a moment. "What makes you believe Gloria could take such a demanding position?"

"I don't know," Haley replied, hoping her tease wouldn't upset him. "The way her eyes light up when you walk in the room. The way sweat beads her brow when you whisk her away on your arm, hoping nobody will see. It's obvious."

"You're a very observant girl," he said, chuckling. "Well, if you must know, I ended our affair just after our last meeting. I mean, I'll admit she's quite the eye-candy, but I just don't have time or the patience to see someone else's wife. Not to mention the dollar signs in her eyes. My word, I really feel sorry for Richard. The poor bastard's heading for bankruptcy."

The mention of Richard's name made her shiver slightly, and she hoped he didn't see her reaction.

"Listen," he said, cocking his head to the side. "I know I haven't been on the straight and narrow, thanks to my father, of course. But I am trying to legitimize his business. I want to make it worth something in the real world. It's a lot more work for me, but the mines I've obtained in Africa and Mexico are working out, slowly, mind you, but it's getting easier to manage."

"So," he continued. "I'm hoping you'll not only be my assistant, but my personal bodyguard as well. You'll go with me wherever I go. It's not like I have a hit on my head, but it'd be nice knowing you're there." A hint of innocence showed in his excitement. "Have you ever seen Bridal Veil Falls from the ground? It's absolutely breathtaking!"

He simmered in his excitement and then touched her face once more. The grin he gave seemed sweet, but still, there was a lingering scheme in his eyes.

"Take a few weeks to think about my offer, relax and enjoy a vacation for once. When you decide, come to my house on the coast and spend a few days with me." He handed her a sleek black business card with a phone number printed in gold. "If you feel you'd rather not take the job I'm offering, I'll let you go."

"Let me go?" she asked, curious of his expression as she slid the card from his fingers.

"I assure you," he continued as he strode to the door, pulling her with him by the hand. "You'll love your new place. You're an advantageous woman who desires action. South Africa, Mexico, they aren't the safest places in the world. I'd feel safer with you there—rather, my life in your hands, and vice versa, of course."

He raised her hand to his lips, eyes on hers. With a quick bow, he kissed the back of her palm, and then moved his lips to the inside of her wrist.

"I'll give you everything your heart desires—money, power, love. Whatever you want, beautiful, it'll be yours."

He was a charmer indeed. It was almost hard to believe he was this despicable drug dealer the cops labeled him to be. She decided for now she'd give him the benefit of the doubt until the time came he showed his ugly self.

She watched him walk down the corridor, strutting with hands in his pockets, whistling as if nothing fazed him in the least. Her suspicious eyes watched as he turned the corner and disappeared from sight, followed by his frowning cronies.

"What did you two talk about?" Shane whispered in her ear, startling her from behind.

She scowled, trying to catch her breath as she made her way back to the porch. "Don't ever sneak up on me like that again!" she said through clenched teeth.

She sat on the edge of the chair, resting her elbows on her knees. She sensed Shane's curiosity.

"He invited me to his house on the coast for a few days to see about a job," she said in a low voice, almost a whisper. "He wants me to be his assistant or personal bodyguard, or something."

Shane turned on his foot and planted his rear-end on the arm of the chair she sat in. He leaned close.

"You accepted, right?" he asked, keeping his voice low as if someone were listening.

"It doesn't feel right," she confessed. "It seems too coincidental, too planned."

"Why do you say that?"

"He says he's trying to legitimize the business, but I don't know. I think he suspects something, so he's lying."

Shane shook his head. But as he was about to speak, Jordan appeared in the doorway.

"Haley," he announced. "The Bossman wants us all in the dining room for some big announcement."

"We're on our way," she replied coolly.

As soon as he disappeared, she returned her attention to Shane. Standing up, she opened her mouth to talk but he silenced her with an immediate kiss.

It happened so fast she couldn't deny him. He held her close for moments, indulging in it, giving her everything he had emotionally, physically. And when he broke from her lips, he growled playfully. "I just had to know," he said.

"Know what?" she asked, trying to regain her composure.

"I saw the kiss you gave him," he said as he walked past her. "You looked like you enjoyed it."

She followed him out and fell into pace behind him. Was he jealous? If he only knew she'd thought of him during the kiss.

They walked into the quiet dining room. Her eyes went straight to Devin who stood at the head of the table. Ignoring the cold mean looks from her partners, she sat down in one of the chairs and gave him her attention.

"I want you all to be clear on this," Devin finally said, glancing around the room, but placing his eyes on Haley for more than a moment. "What happened last night won't be held against any of you. Mistakes happen no matter how professional a team is. The only thing you can do is find the courage to continue."

Haley saw relief in her team's eyes. None of them had ever met Devin before, and she could tell they were already taken with him. Everyone except Trevor, who looked at his hands folded on the table. His face was too complex to read.

"Regardless, I'm making changes starting tomorrow," Devin continued, gathering Haley's attention back on him. "Trevor will be in charge here until further notice."

First time for everything, Haley thought as Trevor's face suddenly went blank. He gazed at her with questioning eyes, asking her what she was going to do. And as if Devin read his mind, he answered.

"Haley's moving into the house on the coast. She'll be my personal assistant from now on. I imagine she'll do a little bodyguard work as well."

She hadn't decided yet, though it was already decided for her from both the cops and Devin. She'd learned not to talk back to anyone in a position above her, but for some reason she couldn't help opening her mouth.

"I haven't …"

"I accept the position. Thank you." Trevor suddenly stood up, interrupting her. He flashed a stern eye her way, but released it quickly to look at the others. "I imagine none of you have any gripes over me taking leadership."

Haley could see plain as day how happy Sara was she was leaving. They'd been friends once, back before Frank came into the picture. But now here she sat with bitter hatred and frustration, and just plain old jealousy in her eyes.

Devin stood smugly in the doorway. He gave Haley a wink and mouthed the words, "See you later, beautiful."

Haley nodded and watched him turn and leave. If only she were gutsy enough to pull out her gun and shoot him in the back of the head. It'd end this nightmare, this horrible complicated mess she'd gotten herself into.

"Hey," Shane whispered as he walked by. "I'll see you soon."

Haley watched him leave. And the others, including Trevor, departed the room without another glance, leaving her alone with memories.

They'd all been friends at one time. Maybe not close-knit and personal, but they'd meant a great deal to each other. She remembered the way they used to laugh, celebrating after a successful heist. Chase would pop open a bottle of champagne. Or he'd remove the cap on a bottle of aged wine when things went really well. It seemed so long ago.

"This is ridiculous," she scolded herself as she left the dining table.

When she made it to the door, she sighed, terribly distressed. She was going to miss this place. She wondered what would happen once this ordeal was over. Would she end up on the streets again? Or worse yet, in prison with the rest of her estranged family?

She briefly fought with the door-handle to her room until it finally turned on its own. And when the door swung open, she found Shane standing in the doorway.

He quickly pulled her inside and into his arms, caressing her as if he hadn't seen her in months. And when he closed the door, he locked it.

"I don't think I can do this," she confessed, thinking only of her team. "Will they be sent to prison too?"

He gently stroked her hair. "They understood their choice when they got involved."

"So did I," she said. "What makes me so special?"

"You know the answer to that, Haley," he replied. "Chase pulled you into this life when you were just a kid. You've never known anything else."

"Oh that's right—brainwashed," she retorted.

"You say that lightly. But it's true, you never had a choice. The others knew what was right and wrong."

"How do you know?" she asked as she pulled away from his embrace and made her way to her bed. She sat down, eying him curiously.

He stood before her, gazing down with his arms folded over his broad chest. His cocky grin was gone, and in place of it was the stone cold stare of a cop.

"I know Sara's real name is Julie. She told everyone she was discharged honorably, but she's actually an ex-military flight specialist discharged from the Air Force for stealing a helicopter. Diggs' real name is John Doyle. He has a wife and two children at home and actually owns a small restaurant near the beach. He's an elder at his church. Shall I go on?"

She shook her head, feeling guilty for listening to their personal details. "No."

He leaned down on his knees and grabbed her wrists. "I think you need to hear this. So you'll know the difference between you and them."

"No!" she shouted trying to break free her from his grasp, but he wouldn't let go.

"Jordan's a network administrator at South Beach Bank and Trust. He's in charge of internet security, of all things. Last year he took a trip to Hawaii and got married."

She held her head in her hands. "Stop!"

"We don't know much about Michael," he said, finally letting go of her wrists. "He's a rather chilling puzzle."

He strode to the window and peered out into the darkening sky. As he heaved a sigh, Haley placed her eyes on his back. There was one more person to talk about.

"Ever wonder why Trevor's so protective of you?" he asked and turned to face her. "He also worked for the same dealer who had you."

"That's ridiculous," Haley retorted.

"The dealer sent him to find you when you disappeared. When he found you, he didn't have the heart to take you back. Chase convinced him to stay."

She rose to her feet and began to pace as her earliest memories entered her mind. She'd jumped foster homes like a dog through hoops in a circus, but always found herself back on the streets.

Refusing to sell herself like the other girls, she earned money by taking on a lesser evil—delivering drugs for a notorious dealer. He and his gang provided for her until she literally ran into Chase at the park, pick-pocketing his wallet before she excused herself. She was only twelve when that happened. He'd caught her before she could make a getaway, offering her a choice—take the money in his wallet and get a hot meal for the day, or go home with him and live richly.

She glanced at Shane who watched her relive her memories. Embarrassed of her past, she quickly looked away.

"It seems I'm always apologizing to you," he said softly as he came to stand behind her, squeezing her shoulders gently with his hands. "All I want to do is fill in the void of your life, but I'm afraid for you."

"Afraid?" she asked. "Afraid of what?"

"I'm afraid to tell you the dealer you delivered for was also on Yoshino's payroll as a thief."

"How do you know?"

"Chase. He said the man kept you and a few other children in some rundown apartment building. The other kids were already old enough to choose their ways, but you were still very young, impressionable."

She pulled from his embrace. "You need to leave," she said coolly, keeping her back to him.

"Come on, Haley," he pleaded as he reached out to her, but she quickly moved away. Seeing she wouldn't acknowledge him, he walked to the bedroom door.

She waited until she heard the door close before sitting down on the bed. And as she did, she began to cry, wishing he'd just left everything he knew of her unsaid. She hated her past and despised the humiliation she felt from Chase keeping her in the dark about how long she'd actually been in this organization.

Chapter 11

Haley took one last glance at Chase's mansion. It seemed different now, empty and unloved. It was almost as if it felt the same thing she did as she got in the back of the limousine Devin sent for her.

She wished Shane had come back, at least to tell her everything would be okay. It'd been two weeks since they'd spoken. And as the limo pulled out of the driveway, her heart sank. Maybe he'd never meant to come back. Maybe tossing him out of her room was the last straw before he withdrew from the case and left her for good. She leaned her elbow on the car door, and her chin on her knuckles. With solemn eyes, she stared out the window as they passed through the security gate, and pulled onto the highway.

Her past haunted her as the car carried her through the busy city, along streets she'd frequented as a kid. She'd carried so many drugs, it was a wonder she'd never fallen into that lifestyle. She'd seen it in the eyes of the addicts, the tangled web they'd woven around themselves. But she'd never been innocent, and maybe it was the reason why she'd never picked up the habit. She felt guilty— guilty for providing their addiction, guilty for hating them because of it. And more importantly, she despised herself for feeling sorry for them.

The car pulled around to the side of Devin's mansion and into a large courtyard. When it finally stopped, Haley quickly got out, too impatient to wait for the driver to open her door. She pulled her shoulder bag out of the trunk, and slung it over her shoulder. And with a stern look, she followed the driver to the side entrance where another man waited at the door.

"I'll show you to your room," he said, his voice monotone and unenthused as he turned and started down the hallway.

She followed him on slightly shaky legs. Her duffle bag draped over her shoulder suddenly became heavy as her arms became weak. She took in a deep breath, letting it out quickly when they stopped just before a beautiful wide-spiraled staircase.

The doorman pushed a tiny white button on the wall and a hidden elevator door opened. He stepped in and waited for her, emotionless, patient, but oddly his eyes told different.

As she stepped in beside him, she noticed a twitch in his right eye. He was nervous around her, and with good reason. After all, she was notorious in this organization for being a cold-hearted assassin, but if they only knew how wrong they were.

Without a word, he pushed the button to the second floor and silently sighed when the doors closed. She knew he'd thought ill of her. And since she'd be staying here for awhile, she might as well put his mind at ease and strike up a friendly conversation.

"This is a lovely house," she said as the elevator hummed upward.

He stood quietly. Not even a glance or another waver of his eyes until the door opened to the second floor.

"Follow me," he muttered his demand.

Shrugging off his decision to ignore her, she did as she was told. She stepped out of the elevator and drew in a deep gasping breath. She smiled in wonder, feeling as though she'd stepped into a medieval fairy tale.

Arched ceilings carved in dark gray stone extended down an open corridor like a bridge leading to another part of the house. With an open view of the sparkling, deep blue ocean—it took her breath away.

The doorman led her down the stone walkway. Though she swore she saw a gleam in his eye, she shrugged it off as part of the change of scenery.

He led her to a guest house, a private, smaller rendition of the mansion, obviously meant for her. White sheers waved in the open windows and doors extending around the naturally lit room. It had been quite the walk to get there, but Devin was obviously obliging to her privacy, and for that she was thankful.

"The master of the house will see you at six sharp for dinner," the doorman said, keeping his stern eyes forward. "Take the elevator to the first floor. The dining room is down the hall to your left, and the first door to your right past the grand stairwell. Good day, ma'am."

With a nod she understood, she thanked him. He stole a quick glance as he turned around and headed back down the stone walkway toward the elevator.

Stiff, she thought. But there was more to him than he let on, especially since he carried a sidearm underneath his long white jacket.

She walked to the bed and slung her bag on it, happy to finally have the weight lifted. The room was three times as big as hers, and had a much better view.

The sound of crashing waves hit in her ears as she strode through the sliding glass door and out onto the private patio. She gazed past the sky blue pool to the ocean, catching the scent in her nostrils.

"Beautiful," she said letting her breath out in one relaxing huff.

"Yes, you are."

The voice sent chills up her spine. Recognizing the thick southern accent, she turned around to find Devin leaning against the frame in the open doorway. Dressed in a thin white button-up shirt with sleeves rolled just below his elbow, and a pair of black slacks matching his perfectly groomed hair, he looked more handsome than she remembered.

A grin spread across his perfect face as he joined her on the patio. He leaned his elbow against the banister and sighed.

"I'm glad you accepted my proposal," he said with a glimmer in his eye. "I think you'll like it, although we won't be spending a lot of our time here. I have a business meeting next week in Cancun, and I'll need you there with me." He pulled his fingers lightly across her forearm, but removed them immediately, a small show of affection. "I imagine your passports are in order."

Haley nodded, finding it rather disconcerting to be standing here with him. For so long she'd been taught to respect him, possibly even fear the power this man had. It was too astounding to believe he was bad, and especially now when he looked so calm and friendly. He seemed just an ordinary man as she gazed into his eyes wanting to know the secrets he held behind them. She was bound to find out and bring him and his organization to its knees, but it just didn't seem right.

"You're a mystery to me," he said, running his eyes over her lips.

"Why do you say that?" she asked.

"You despise me, yet here you are acting as if you don't." He straightened his stance and gazed deeply into her eyes. "Don't take me for an ignorant fool, Beautiful. I already know the police asked you to keep an eye on me."

Haley suddenly frowned. Nervousness swept through her as she tried to think of something to say, but she couldn't. Her heart pounded in her ears and a sick feeling billowed in her fluttering stomach.

"I'm sorry," she said as she stood ready to defend herself. "I didn't ..."

Devin pressed his finger to her lips. "Don't worry." He moved his hand up to her face and massaged it sensually. "I know how loyal you are to me. I only hope I can prove to you that I'm not this horrible person they make me out to be." He leaned down and kissed her lightly below her eye. "And maybe you might even learn to love me as I do you. After all, I am changing. I've disassembled the heists. I've legitimized by purchasing mines instead of stealing from them. And I hope soon I'll marry—someone to provide me with an heir."

On that note he slid his hand from her face, and gave her a quick wink before he left her side. "I'll see you at dinner," he called out just before he left through the door.

Haley let out an uneasy gasp and quickly found the patio chair. She sat down, trying to catch her breath as the eeriness of Devin's whistling song carried through the corridor.

Chapter 12

Guests mingled, drinking champagne and chatting over classical music floating throughout the first floor of the mansion. Formally dressed in tuxedos and sparkling gowns, they seemed in uniform, at least to Haley's eyes as she stood at the top of the wide staircase and watched them.

Dinner was supposed to be served at six, and it was ten minutes until. She hadn't expected this many people, but nothing seemed expected anymore.

She descended the stairs, a nervous tremble on her bottom lip when she found the room with their eyes on her. She glanced down at herself to make sure nothing was out of place. Seeing her bosom perfectly tucked inside the low-cut black dress, she sighed in relief.

Maybe it was the string of diamonds around her neck shimmering in the light of the room that caught their eyes. It had definitely caught hers when she'd opened it just a few hours ago. Devin had sent it to her as a gift, and she'd used it as reassurance that he meant her no harm, though she knew he still didn't fully trust her, and for good reason. For now she'd continue to be on his side, playing her part, hoping it wouldn't work into anything more than a job.

She hurried through the crowd of guests to the dining room. Pleased to find it empty, she exhaled and let her false grin fall.

The table was set to receive six people, and she wondered what kind of dinner this was. If it were anything like the dinner parties she'd had with Chase, then conversation would be rather interesting.

As she wondered who the invited guests were, Devin walked in, his eyes wide in allure. The way he stared, running his eyes smoothly over her tight curves, made her feel self-conscious. She greeted him with the same false smile she'd carried just moments before, and that seemed to bring his eyes back to hers.

A light scent of musk hit her senses as he grasped her elbow and pulled her close. He brushed his lips along her cheek to her ear, causing a chill to spread over her skin.

"How could something so deadly be the most beautiful thing in the room?" he asked in a whisper. "Come sit with me at the table." He pulled a chair out for her and she graciously accepted her seat. Nervousness washed over her when he took his seat beside her, offering an enthused glance when two tall, muscular men—twins, no doubt—joined them at the table.

"Haley," Devin said, gathering her attention from the hefty giants, quite possibly seeing the hesitance in her eyes. "I'd like for you to meet John and Chuck. They oversee the shipments at the docks."

She greeted them with a smile, though they didn't return it with one of their own. In fact, they viewed her sternly as if condemning her for reasons of doubt. Not that she blamed them, for she too carried the same look when she met somebody new.

She glanced past the two suspicious, overly-dressed men and found two others entering the dining room. Her heart immediately leapt into her throat. Dressed in a tuxedo, black tie around his thick neck, was Shane. And on his arm was none other than Gloria, smiling in her tight yellow gown sparkling with diamonds—most likely real ones.

Haley caught his eyes, but she quickly looked away, turning her attention on Devin. He didn't seem shocked at all as he watched them sit down in their seats, right across from her.

"You look as lovely as ever, Gloria," he said glancing at Shane then back to her. "Has he been taking good care of you?"

"Oh my, yes." Gloria touched Shane's arm and tittered. "He's such a charming man."

Haley still refused to look at Shane, though she watched Gloria blush with lust. Though angry and rather hurt on the inside, she kept her poise, smiling when she caught Gloria's sudden peculiar attention.

"Is that Pearl?" Her eyes widened as she stared at Haley's throat.

"Yes, Gloria, that's Pearl," Devin replied as the meals were being served.

"Pearl?" Haley asked, touching the necklace with her fingertips.

"Pearl was my mother's name," Devin replied. "My father gave her the necklace you're wearing on their wedding night."

"Tell her how much it's worth, Devin," Gloria snapped. "I'd hate for her to lose such a valuable possession. Of course, it is just a loaner, right?"

Devin grinned sheepishly. "No, Gloria. I gave it to her."

As much as Haley loved making Gloria miserable, she despised the attention. She didn't want anything to do with this necklace, no matter how valuable it was. And she wondered why Devin would give her something so obviously sentimental to him.

She turned her attention to her plate, anxious to get this dinner over with. She couldn't wait to get back to her room and take her aggressions out on the punching bag, conveniently hanging in the corner of the retreat. She couldn't wait to soak herself in the Jacuzzi next to the pool, somewhat relaxing the tension in her body. And she desperately couldn't wait to get out from beneath Shane's stare.

"There are going to be major changes in the company," Devin spoke loud and clear as he wiped the corners of his mouth with his napkin. "Chuck, John—I invited you here to instruct you on how clean," he emphasized the word, "the warehouse needs to be. Everything implicating my business needs to be eliminated. I've cut ties to all existing overseas cargo to make way for the new, legitimate goods. So from now on, the only shipments coming in should be from our mines in Mexico and South Africa."

"Sir?" Chuck looked puzzled, but he nodded when he saw Devin's serious expression.

"My father's been dead for six years," he said. "I've been meaning to do this for a while, but it's taken me this long to learn all the aspects of his business. I'm confident enough to begin cleaning up his mess, starting with the overseas shipments of stolen jewels."

Haley glanced at Shane, wondering if he couldn't arrest him now. After all, it was a confession. But of course, the warehouse would be clean way before the cops could raid. Then there would be no evidence to bring him in.

"Richard was the overseer of that department, but I've moved him elsewhere. Unfortunately, I need him in Mexico rather than in the States. He asked me to invite you here, Gloria—to explain why he's been absent for the past few days."

All eyes were on him. And whether it made him nervous or not, he didn't show it. Always cool, collected, he went about eating again without a twitch, and without acknowledging Gloria's determined look.

Haley turned her puzzled eyes on Shane as if asking him what she was supposed to do. Was Devin acting, or was he speaking the truth about his will to change? But Shane's attention went immediately to Gloria, smiling with his eyes and giving her his full attention. And furthermore, he didn't seem surprised or concerned to hear Devin's announcement.

Haley's dinner sat untouched, having lost her appetite when Shane first walked into the room. Jealousy wasn't part of her nature, but this situation was really getting to her. With Richard out of the picture, who knows what that woman was making him do?

"Your home is here now, Haley," Devin said, interrupting her distressing thoughts. "You'll always have a home with me."

"Oh, you've got to be kidding!" Gloria snapped, then threw her napkin down on her plate and stormed off to the open balcony.

Devin tossed a rather embarrassed but flattered glance. "Excuse me," he said as he stood on his feet and walked out to join Gloria.

Haley felt Shane's gaze on her. Though he said no words, she could tell he beckoned her to look at him, and she did. His look was stern, serious as he stared into her eyes. What was this look for?

She couldn't help but glare at him. Anger and hurt masked the curiousness of his presence, but she was quickly cured when she heard Chuck's deep, troubling voice.

"I've heard a lot about you, Haley," he said. "You're a celebrity in the organization, you know."

"It's fitting for you to take his side," John said as he stood up, glass of champagne in hand. "Just watch your back when you go to either of the mines."

"What do you mean?" she asked, slightly annoyed when he touched her on the shoulder.

"Call the people superstitious, but these new mine workers don't like Devin much," Chuck said as he too stood on his feet, glass in hand. "Devin's last assistant took a bullet in the head just after his plane arrived. The worker who shot him claimed the assistant to be the right hand of Diablo."

Haley didn't know what to think. Were they giving her advice, or was this some kind of warning? It didn't matter; she knew she could handle herself and protect Devin if she had to.

Shane suddenly looked worried, but he hid it when Gloria ran through the room and out into the hallway, tears streaming down her pretty pale face. He sighed when he stood up. And with one last warning glance at Haley, he hurried out to find her.

Devin returned to the table. He nodded at Chuck and John, and thanked them for coming. And without another glance, they left the room to join the party outside.

"I'm sorry about that," he said with a chuckle. "Gloria has it in her mind that she was meant for me and Pearl as well."

Haley glanced down at the necklace. It dazzled brilliantly in the light, but it still carried no significance for her. She'd rather not wear it, or better yet, not have it at all.

"I appreciate your gift," she said. "But don't you think it's much too valuable to give to me? After all, it was your mother's."

"True," he said, leaning back in his chair. "I shouldn't be surprised that you don't like it."

"Oh, I do. It's beautiful."

"But?" he asked.

She found the courage to look at him, discretion in her glance. "But I've never been one for material possessions, especially items making other people jealous."

He watched her unclasp the necklace. "You amaze me with your candor. There aren't many women like you in the world. I truly respect that." She carefully handed him Pearl. "I think that's what I love most about you, Haley. You remind me of my mother. She was a lovely woman, strong and capable of taming the fiercest beast. My father was brutal, but she had him wrapped tight around her finger."

"What happened to them?"

Devin sighed. "She discovered some truly horrific things about him and tried to leave, but of course he wouldn't allow it. Once you're in the company, you're in for life. She tried to talk to me, but I was too stubborn to care what the bastard did, so I didn't listen."

"What kind of horrific things?"

He hesitated, but a grin spread across his handsome face as he stood up with an outstretched hand. She could tell the conversation had ended.

"Let's go out and join the party," he said. "I would love to dance with you, if you don't mind."

She accepted his hand and he helped her to her feet. He tucked her arm under his and led her out into the noisy room, gathering the guests' curious eyes.

People looked at him with utmost respect, as they should, and he accepted their greetings with a gracious bow of his head. He was king of this house, this powerful organization, so if any ill will went his way, it wasn't showing tonight.

Light classical played throughout the rooms, and voices carried with laughter and talk. Haley actually began to enjoy dancing. It helped that Devin could dance wonderfully, leading her gently. And for a brief moment, she couldn't believe he was this terrifying monster they'd warned her about.

Someone suddenly tapped on her shoulder, rather forcefully. She knew without looking who interrupted the dance, and caused Devin to frown. But Haley graciously let go of his hand, letting him know it was alright.

"I'm cutting in," Gloria announced, barely giving her enough time to step away as she slid in between her and Devin.

"I'll be right back, Beautiful," Devin said in a regretful voice as he grabbed Gloria by the wrist and led her down the hall toward the kitchen.

Haley suddenly felt awkward, standing alone in the middle of the other dancers who watched her, as they had most of the night. She headed for the stairs, anxious to return to her room, but a strong hand caught her.

With a quick yank, Shane pulled her into his arms and began dancing with her, forcing his lead. His muddy eyes sparkled as he stared into hers, and then brushed her hair over her shoulder with an electric touch.

Though it felt so right, she couldn't forget how angry she was. She left his arms, eager to get to her room and away from him. She ascended the stairs quickly and walked down the hall to the elevator. She stepped inside and pushed the button to her floor. But when she believed she'd escaped, he stepped in behind her just in time for the elevator to close them in.

Not a word came from him, but she felt his pleading eyes. She wanted to confess how angry she was with him, but all she could do was stand there quietly until the elevator lifted to her floor.

As soon as the door opened, she stepped out. She walked fast down the dark walkway, hoping to get to her room before he stopped her, but it was too late. He grabbed her by the hand and twisted her around.

She stared into his eyes for an angry moment, feeling warmth in her cheeks. The gentle wind propelled her hair, tickling her scowling face. But the sound of the waves crashing in the distance seemed to wash the anger away, bringing hurt feelings to the surface.

"Leave me alone," she whispered.

"You don't mean that," he said in a deep, serious tone. "I know you're upset with me, but please let me explain."

"Don't tell me where you've been for two weeks. I don't need your excuses."

"They're not excuses."

She turned to leave him, but he caught her again by the wrist. He forcefully turned her around to face him, this time pressing her hard against him.

"I'm sorry," he whispered. "I couldn't decline the babysitting job, or I'd be under suspicion." He gently massaged the back of her head. "But if I would've known it would hurt you like this, I would have asked to be placed somewhere else."

"Don't be ridiculous. I'm fine with it."

She took hold of his wrists and removed his hands from her head. With an understanding smile, she released herself from his hold and leaned forward against the stone banister.

"You're not fine, Haley."

The moon lit up the night, shimmering over the ocean. As she watched and listened, she felt his hands slide over her back and come to rest on her shoulders.

"When I saw you with her, I thought ..." She paused to stand upright, facing him. "I thought you and she—"

"Believe me. We have absolutely no interest in each other. She's got it bad for Devin." He chuckled. "He's all that woman talks about, even in front of Richard."

Haley frowned at the mention of Richard. "I never thought I'd ever wish he were here," she retorted. "I can't stand seeing her near you."

"It's necessary," he replied. "As much as I love your jealousy, I have to be honest. This is the first time I've ever been anywhere with Gloria. Richard made me come while he went off to Mexico for a few days. His exact words were, 'Don't let her spend big while I'm gone.'" He chuckled. "Personal bodyguard to his finances, I'd say. I was supposed to be in Mexico."

"Shane," Haley whispered. "He knows."

He looked at her curiously. "What do you mean he knows?"

She shook her head, feeling as though her world was about to fall apart. Should she tell him about Devin's knowledge of her involvement with the cops? If she did, it might ruin everything they'd worked for. He still seemed to trust her, so she couldn't take the risk Shane would call off the act. And she knew he would.

"I meant, he believes I care about him," she said. "He confessed he loves me."

"Just be careful," he said with a sudden frown. "If he lays one finger on you, I'll—"

"You'll what?" she interrupted. "You can't do anything about it, Shane. You'll be somewhere else slapping Gloria's hand when she reaches inside her purse."

The frustration in his face turned to pain. His skin turned a faint shade of red in the pale moonlight. It would have showed a much deeper shade in sunlight.

"You know I can take care of myself."

"Can you?" he asked. "What happens when he wants to take you to bed and you refuse? The man doesn't understand rejection. He'll force the issue."

"He's not like that, Shane. He's been very much a gentleman toward me. I just can't believe he's this horrible person you make him out to be. He seems to genuinely want to change, make things legit. Regardless of what he's done in his past, I at least respect him for that."

Shane suddenly took a step back, stunned by her words. "Respect him? Haley," he swallowed hard and continued, "After everything I've told you about him, you actually like him?"

She stood rigid before him, confident. The serious look she

gave outweighed the gentle touch of her hand on his arm. And he quickly pulled away, realizing her answer was 'yes'.

"You can't be serious!" he shouted followed by a string of profanities. He turned away, walking—pacing as he breathed fast, trying to control his flaring temper.

"Let me explain," she said as she swore she saw steam roll off his body. He slammed his fists down on the stone and grabbed the edge.

"What's there to explain?" he asked angrily, taking a few steps toward her. His voice was strained as tension moved through his body. "It's your job to get close, but you're not supposed to get personally involved." He straightened his body and gazed inquiringly. "Exactly how involved are you?"

"Shane," she said.

"You had sex with him." He tossed her a perturbed glance after his assumption.

"That's not fair," she retorted, more hurt than angry over his choice of words. "You know I would never."

"When you come running to me after he's messed you up, I'm not going to be there."

"Would you just listen to me? I—"

"I've heard enough," he said as he headed toward the elevator. "We need to get back to the party before they notice we're gone."

"No," she said, refusing to move. "I'm not leaving until you listen to what I have to say."

He turned for a moment, gave her a quick disappointed glance and then turned his eyes to the floor. "Suit yourself. But I'm leaving."

She watched him get inside the elevator, the hurt on his face abundant. She was shocked, appalled he'd thrown such a tantrum without listening. He had it all wrong. She didn't want to make her bed with Devin, but she definitely wanted him to believe it.

Chapter 13

Haley leaned against the window in the dark garage watching as people left the party in their fancy cars and limos. She envied them, wishing she could go home as well. But then again, she was home for now, at least until Devin was behind bars. And then after that? Who knew where she'd belong. The thought disturbed her.

But Devin had accepted her, trusted her even though she'd lied to him about her involvement with the police. He invited her to live with him, to take care of her, and she knew he would in every way if she allowed it.

Maybe it wouldn't be so bad. He was rather handsome and quite generous with his feelings. He'd never said a harsh word or showed any aggression toward anyone since she'd met him. So maybe he was serious about legitimizing the business.

She sighed, returning her thoughts to Shane. Her heart beat a little faster. She remembered the hurt in his face when he thought she'd been with Devin and it had stuck with her all evening. He was a jerk for not letting her get in her explanation, but it was exactly how she'd felt when he walked in with Gloria.

She left through the door and walked across the busy courtyard. Cigar smoke caught her attention, and it reminded her of Chase. He'd enjoyed a cigar most evenings in his study, and every once in a great while, she'd joined him.

She missed him terribly. If she ever needed advice on something, this was it. What was she supposed to do? As she entered the house, pushing by a group of leaving guests, she thought of what he'd say. "Listen to your instincts. You know Devin is vindictive, a player in all aspects of the word. Once you're in, you're in for life. Just watch your back and don't get too close."

It's exactly what Chase would say, and they were words well

taken. But she was already in for life and the only way to get out was to bring Devin down. And the only way to bring him down was to get close. And the closer she got to him, the more she liked him.

"There you are," Devin said as he entered the hall from the dining room. He took her by the hand and led her up the stairs. "You look troubled, beautiful. Is something wrong?"

"No," she answered, hoping she hadn't sounded too hasty. "I'm fine."

He watched her as he led her slowly down the long hall. "If you have a problem with Gloria staying here while Richard's gone, please let me know. I'll send her home right away."

She was surprised to hear this news, but hid it well under her slight grin. This meant Shane would be staying, too.

"I'm fine, really. I think I'm just a little tired is all."

"Did you pick out a car?" he asked as he led her through the double doors at the end of the hall. He grasped her hand and whisked her around to face him as he shut the doors with his foot. Haley was suddenly aware of her surroundings and cleared her throat, noticing his large bed. Candles were lit around the room casting a soft glow on the walls. Their pungent flower scent permeated the air, making her strangely dizzy.

"The black spider ..." Her breath suddenly became erratic. Her fingers pressed against her temple as the room began to spin.
Devin led her to the bed and sat her down. "Are you okay?" he asked, taking her hands in his. "Maybe you should lie down."

This wasn't good. He'd obviously brought her here to woo her into bed. She definitely wasn't ready for this. But then again, maybe feeling rather nauseous was a good thing, giving her an excuse to decline him without fearing what he'd do over rejection.

She inched her way back to the pillow and lay down, groaning lightly. "I'm sorry," she said in a breath.

"Well," he replied sweetly. "It's not how I imagined our first night together." He leaned over her, kissed her forehead, and then chuckled. "But at least I got you in bed."

She didn't know whether to laugh or not. He sounded like he might be teasing, but his face remained stern. He sat down beside her and held her, stroking her head as if she were a cat until she fell asleep.

•

It felt like she'd closed her eyes only for a moment when daylight streamed through the open doors of the balcony. The bed she lay on was soft—comfortable to a point she didn't want to leave it. But when she saw Devin standing outside, gazing at the ocean scenery, she suddenly remembered where she was.

She quickly rose from the bed and straightened the wrinkles from her dress. She found her heeled shoes on the floor, peeking out from beneath the red fabric of the bed skirt. Frantic to get back to her own room, she pulled them out. But she stopped before she slipped them on remembering her place. This was exactly where she was supposed to be.

After running her fingers through her somewhat tousled hair, and tossing a quick glance in the round antique mirror on the wall, she picked up her shoes and joined Devin on the balcony. She slid in beside him, taking in the same ocean scenery he'd been watching. And then she felt his eyes on her, quickly gathering her attention.

"Did you sleep well?"

"Yes," she replied. "Thank you for letting me stay."

"Well, I don't think I had a choice in the matter." He chuckled as he brushed a lock of her hair over her shoulder. "Next time I'll make sure the candles aren't lit, hmm?"

It was odd the way he changed his entire appearance, straightening his stance and tightening his lips into a straight line. He almost glared.

"I need you with me at the warehouse this morning," he said in a much deeper, more serious tone. "It seems Richard arrived with a new shipment this morning. The idiot brought the overseers from the mine with him. Apparently they're looking for an advance in our contract."

"When are we leaving?" she asked, dropping her shoes and slipping them on her feet.

"Be ready in an hour," he said, his tenor coming back as he watched her rise an inch in her heels. "You're so beautiful."

She turned to leave before he made a pass. "We only have an hour."

She walked out and shut the door behind her. With quickness in her step, she made her way down the long hallway. She checked her watch—ten a.m. If she needed to be ready by eleven then she needed to move a little faster. But when she looked up to find her way to the elevator, she ran straight into Gloria, shadowed by Shane who looked as pale as a ghost. Realizing they'd both witnessed her leaving Devin's room, in the same outfit she wore the previous night, she picked up the pace.

"Excuse me," she said as she passed them and headed toward the elevator. It would have been too easy to get away without a confrontation as Shane fell into stride beside her.

"What happened?" he said through clenched teeth.

"Nothing," she replied as she stepped inside the elevator and turned to face him.

"Did you sleep with him?"

"I'm not answering that question when you already know the answer," she said.

"So you're choosing his side then."

She looked at him before she pushed the button to the second floor. The same hurt she saw last night lingered again. She thought maybe she should tell him the truth, but then this was satisfying her desire for payback over his degrading assumption.

"I don't know what I'm going to do yet," she said as the elevator doors shut on his bemused face. "I'll decide once I see his intentions."

Chapter 14

Haley knew what she was doing, at least she hoped. She followed Devin into the warehouse and shivered slightly. Sunglasses shaded her eyes, hiding unsure emotions from unwanted glances. If they were to look, they'd only see seriousness, fearlessness—maybe even a little vexation.

She dared anyone to start a fight. The punching bag in her room didn't hold a candle to hitting the real thing. In play or a real scrap, the exhilaration of a good fight was almost as good as sex. And winning? That was just orgasmic.

Haley tucked away her thoughts as they walked through the room of crates, the shipment from Mexico. She desperately wanted to see what was inside. But she figured in due time she'd get her chance, maybe tonight during a late night break in.

Haley followed Devin into a small room at the back of the warehouse where they found Richard sitting in a high-back cushioned chair. He looked bad—real bad, like he'd been sick for months without care. It served him right, though he deserved much worse.

"Richard," Devin spoke with a motivated tone. "You look unwell."

"Devin," Richard replied in a raspy voice. "You remember Rodriguez, don't you?"

"Yes," Devin replied as he stretched out his hand, offering the short Spanish man, standing at the edge of the desk, a friendly shake. "I trust your trip on my freighter was rather interesting."

Rodriguez grinned in a friendly way and then shook his hand as if he'd known him for years—an old friend. As he began talking about his trip, and how uncomfortable the bed was, Haley scanned the room.

Eight tall gray file cabinets lined the back windowed wall, each drawer labeled in alphabetic organization, with one exception. The end cabinet had no labels and its top drawer was open and empty. Beside it sat a cardboard box full of folders carelessly tossed inside possibly meant to be thrown away, perhaps part of the cleansing Devin ordered his twin overseers.

She scanned the ceiling and walls with her eyes—no cameras. It'd be easy to break in unnoticed, as long as no night security threatened it. She skimmed the floor and found four large dishes sitting next to the desk … dogs.

She had no problems making her way around people silently. But dogs, especially big ones, she had a problem with. Though it might alter her plans a bit, she knew she had to find out what information they had here, just to get this ridiculous act over with and move on with her life, wherever that led.

She watched Devin as he made chit-chat with Rodriguez. She was perfectly comfortable standing here beside him. As he began reading the shipping invoice of precious gems with his new acquaintance, and Richard, who looked more peaked by the minute. She couldn't help but like him. Indeed she could get used to being with him, protecting him from anyone who meant him harm.

Her eyes immediately fell on Rodriguez. There was something off about him. Maybe it was the way he shifted his eyes to the floor, the desk, the warehouse … the exit door. She'd stay on guard.

Diamonds, rubies, even gold bars supposedly sat in the crates in the warehouse, perfect for an ambush of wrongdoers. With such minimal security, it'd be an easy target, especially for criminals like Haley's former group. This would be a walk in the park for them.

Devin suddenly took her by the hand. Even though she'd heard him say he wanted to take a look at the goods, his touch startled her. He led her out into the warehouse where four very fit men joined Rodriguez. They followed uniformly, making her incredibly nervous.

"As you know, each crate has a unique code," Rodriguez said slowly, struggling with his English. "You will find the codes on the manifest."

He took the position next to the large metal crate and punched in a series of numbers on the security pad, which unlocked the door. He opened the double doors and waited for Devin.

Devin didn't hesitate as he let go of Haley's hand and walked in. His trust in this character was more than she'd wanted. Of course, she wouldn't budge, staying outside with the four brute bodyguards.

"Beautiful!" Devin said loudly, obviously impressed with the goods. "We agreed on a price, correct?"

"Three hundred large," Rodriguez replied.

Haley imagined her face went pale. This was supposed to be a shipment of precious gems—a planned shipment. This was supposed to be a negotiation of an advance, but what it sounded like to her was a drug deal going down. She couldn't panic, not in front of these men.

Devin responded quickly. "I've already bought once from your company at one-seventy-five. I agreed at a firm two due to economic reasons. Why the sudden jump in price?"

A moment went by in silence. The four men Haley stood with glanced at each other briefly, obviously not realizing this turn of events. Luckily, it was only temporary.

"I agreed on two with condition. You have offered us no safety here in this unguarded warehouse."

Haley heard Devin chuckle, and then suddenly he came out of the crate, pulling Rodriguez with him.

The four bodyguards stepped in front of him, keeping him from moving any further with their boss—loyal dogs. But Rodriguez waved them away, though the puzzled look on his face told them to stay close behind. And Haley fell into pace right along with them.

"I only want to put your mind at ease," Devin said as he led him up the side stairwell toward the roof. "You'll find your stay here quite secure and very hospitable."

When they reached the roof, they made their way to the bay side. Devin pointed down near a group of crates between warehouses. A long black car was parked near the entrance, and inside sat two men dressed in black suits.

"You'll see the same security around these warehouses. And if you look close enough, you might even spot a few guns on the rooftops." Devin lowered his brow. "Now, Rodriguez, I highly doubt you have any say in the matter of safety. I imagine you'll take my offer of two hundred thousand per crate. And if you keep your visit pleasant, I might add a bonus to our transactions."

His eyes—she couldn't help but get lost in their dark lure, the unbelievable demand in them. Blue had never looked so beautiful, so frightening. She shivered.

Rodriguez was no fool as he accepted Devin's proposal with a nod. There was no doubt he saw the same intent in his eyes. And he was obviously very intimidated.

"Then we have a deal," Devin continued without question as he led everyone back inside.

When they returned to the office, Richard set a black briefcase on the table. Devin immediately opened it without glancing at the contents inside.

"I've never had problems parting with money until now," he said as he eyed Rodriguez. "My only warning to you is there better be a profitable return on this investment."

"I—I promise your customer will be generous," Rodriguez stammered. "I've dealt with him for more than twenty years. He will be good for your operation."

Haley stood next to Devin. Every word spoken sounded like innuendo, and most assuredly was. Regardless, she still wanted to give Devin benefit of the doubt. At least until she discovered for herself, making plans for tonight to break in and see what all this was about. Hopefully, everything was still here and completely legitimate as Devin pledged.

Rodriguez picked up the briefcase. Haley saw a shiver work through him, though he hid it well from the other eyes in the room. After a quick nod, he dismissed himself, followed by his glaring thugs.

And then Devin sighed, not in relief, but in absolute irritation as he sat on the edge of the desk and turned his attention to Richard. "Gloria moved into my house. I'm sure you'll work on moving her to your new place in Cancun. I doubt it'll take much convincing since your place is nothing short of a resort."

Haley heard Richard grumble slightly with his eyes closed. He almost looked as though he slept sitting up in his chair with his arms folded over his chest, chin tucked down. And then Devin spoke the exact words she'd just thought.

"Go see a doctor, Richard, before you keel over in my warehouse."

Devin turned to Haley and his irritation melted. He stood up and palmed her face with a gentle glance, one much different than before. He seemed trusting, as if, for some reason, he was quite pleased with her.

"I'm taking you to dinner tonight," he blurted, ignoring Richard's sudden glower. "I promise we'll dine alone—no meetings. It'll just be you and me getting to know each other a bit more—" His voice trailed as he took off her sunglasses so he could see her eyes. "Intimately."

"Are you mad?" Richard asked in his raspy voice. He cleared his throat with a cough and then swallowed hard. "You can't get close to her! She's working for—"

"Quiet you old fool," Devin interrupted his last words. "I know where her true loyalty lies, regardless of who tries to coax her. She's with me. And really now, I have nothing to hide anymore."

Haley knew Richard's last words were "the police." She wondered just how far this information had traveled. Had it gone through the entire organization? If it had, then she might have to look over her shoulder more often.

Devin looked into her eyes with an odd expression. It was as if he searched her soul for a fear she'd hidden deep inside, but his words expressed something quite different.

"You can have your wish if you desire it," he whispered low enough only for her ears. "I don't need him."

She let his words roll around in her head. It took a moment to decipher, but when she figured it out, her eyes grew wide. This was something she didn't expect, especially now.

She glanced at Richard. His pale, overburdened face turned down again. His eyes were closed, resting in his sickened state. He was weak, pathetic, as he sat unaware of the conversation, oblivious of what could happen to him if she were to act on such a heinous, but deserving crime. She could easily and quickly snap his neck, and he'd never see it coming.

She returned her eyes to Devin's. She grew suspicious and surprisingly a touch hurt. "Is that an order?" she whispered, playing his game.

"Never," he said aloud, taken back by her question, obviously not expecting it. "I'll never make you do anything you don't want to."

His words didn't put her mind at ease. It should have, but it only made her feel tense and unsure. If he truly trusted her, he would give the order. And in her recollection of the organization, once the boss wanted someone removed, they were removed.

She suddenly felt sorry for Richard knowing it would only be a matter of time before he was dismissed. She knew she shouldn't feel bad for the bastard, but she couldn't help it. Maybe before she'd become involved with Shane, she never would have felt pity. This was his fault. He'd made her weak-minded, emotional. The sensitive woman she'd buried most of her life had come to the surface only because of him. She hated him for this, but damn did her heart sink at the mere thought of him.

"You look angry," Devin said as he led her through the warehouse. "I didn't mean to upset you. I only thought maybe you'd like to hurt him a little for what he made you do to Chase."

"I did what was asked of me. Chase is dead. I've accepted it," Haley said in a cold tone. "Revenge isn't really my forte."

"You're an amazing woman," he said as he led her to the car outside. He got in first and then held out his hand. "Ride with me?"

Haley looked at the Spider she'd driven to the warehouse. As much as she hated leaving it parked there, she gathered she could use it as an excuse in case she got caught here tonight. Of course, she'd never get caught. And on that note, she took Devin's hand and got inside the car.

Chapter 15

Devin cancelled dinner due to a "situation," as he called it. Haley heard him speaking to Gloria, who looked unusually worried. Apparently Richard had checked himself into the hospital after the meeting at the warehouse, and the doctors had diagnosed him with pneumonia.

Though Haley was a little disappointed she'd miss dinner out for a change, she was relieved she didn't have to come up with an excuse to end the evening short. And as she watched Devin's car leave the driveway heading for the hospital, she breathed a relieving sigh.

It felt like months since she'd relaxed. Ever since Richard first came to her about the hit on Chase, she'd been overstressed, unable to focus on herself. She had always found time to unwind, no matter what job she was on or how tough things got.

Haley stepped inside the elevator, wanting desperately not to cry. It was nothing more than a weakness, and she wasn't weak. She looked at her reflection in the mirror. A pitiful woman stared back. Dark rings shaded her skin beneath cold glaring eyes. She despised her, almost as much as she hated the act she'd been forced to play. It would be so easy to run away and never look back. But then again, which would be weaker—the tear-filled woman or the fake? The elevator door opened to the dark corridor. She stepped out and studied the thick fog in the archways that created a mystical, unclear path to her room. And standing just before the mist was Shane.

"What are you doing here?" she asked as she stepped out of the elevator, remembering the last time they'd spoke. It was just that morning he'd accused her of sleeping with Devin.

Shane watched as she walked past him though her glance

stayed forward. He didn't say a word, but she sensed he'd fell into pace behind her. And though she was still angry with him, she couldn't help but be comforted by his presence. Maybe it was the fog clouding her judgment.

"Haley, stop," he said as the door to her room came in sight. She pulled the key from her pocket as she turned to face him, but her gaze turned to the side. She'd lose herself if she met his eyes. He was angry anyway. And the only way she could accept it is if she kept from looking at him.

"What do you want?" she asked, damning her peripheral vision. With it, she watched him come closer. And when he took her hand, it sent an electrical shock straight through her. She'd forgotten how his touch affected her, taking an instant breath. She forced herself to back away.

He quickly caught her hand, and this time pulled her close. "I'm sorry about earlier. It's not my place to pry into your life. It's just; when you're with him, I can't stand the thought, Haley. I don't want to see you get hurt."

She finally found courage to look at him. He looked sincere and absolutely stunning. Did he really believe she'd fallen for Devin rather than take his side?

She turned to the door and unlocked it. She felt his hand slide from hers as she walked inside, but her quick reflex caught it. She pulled him into the room and shut the door, locking it behind her, and then turned to face him once again. This time she looked him straight in the eye.

"I'm not with him, Shane," she said as she moved closer to him. "I've been with you from the beginning of this and I'll see it through no matter what I have to do."

"No," he said shaking his head. His voice grew stern, unapologetic. "I never asked you to sleep with him, not for the sake of this investigation, and definitely not against your will. I would never ask you to do such a thing. I'm angry at myself for letting it happen. I never wanted you to ..."

"Shut up," she interrupted, covering his mouth with her hand. She pressed her body against his and then slid her hands over his broad shoulders. "I didn't sleep with him. I fell asleep in his bed, alone. That's all that happened."

She slid her hands across his chest and then up to his face. She tried to pull him closer, close enough to press her lips to his but he caught her wrists.

"What are you doing, Haley?"

"Do you have to ask?"

"Yes," he said, holding fast to keep her from touching him.

She held her confused look for a moment, and then released it angrily. "Then let go of me."

"Not until you answer me," he said as she began to struggle. "Were you trying to kiss me?" A sudden mischievous grin fell across his face.

"No," she lied, sensing his tease. "I'm not in the mood for games."

She twisted her body around and quickly threw him over on the floor on his back, forcing him to let go of her wrists. But as if he'd expected her to perform such a stunt, he caught her by the waist before she could escape. He pulled her down beside him and then pinned her beneath his body, holding her tight to the floor.

"Let me up!" she said between clenched teeth, struggling to get him off, but he wouldn't budge. And though he wasn't crushing the breath from her, it was quite uncomfortable.

"You remember this move?" he asked as he pressed his knees slightly against her legs. "I could easily paralyze you and leave you here alone. Or worse yet, if I were a bad guy, I could take advantage of the situation."

She glared at him. "I don't need a lesson in defending myself. I can easily get you off. But unlike you, I don't want to hurt you."

"I'm not trying to hurt you, Haley," he said. "But you're right; I am trying to get you to understand how serious this is. Devin isn't an idiot. He'll see right through your act if you try to get too close without giving him what he wants. And we both know what he wants."

"I don't need a lecture either," she said with a scowl. "I know what I'm doing."

"Do you?" he asked as if surprised. "If you're so confident, then please, try to get out of my hold."

"I don't want to hurt you."

"I'm giving you permission. Hurt me," he said with a half-grin.

He was completely serious. For a moment she pondered the thought, knowing he wouldn't let up until she at least tried. The problem with her escape was that she'd get hurt too, enough to impair her for a few moments. But if it meant proving to him she could take care of herself, then she'd have to do it.

"On the count of three," he said as he saw the decision in her blank face. "One. Two. Thr—"

With all her effort, she pulled her body up. It was a split second decision as she pressed her lips to his when she'd meant to hit his nose with her head. Thankfully he kissed her back, releasing her wrists. She threw her arms around his neck as he lifted her up from the floor.

She wrapped her legs around his waist as he carried her to the bed, frantically undressing her. Their lips moved together as each piece of clothing fell to the floor. And when he pulled his body over hers, a thunderous boom made them both suddenly stop.

"What was that?" Haley asked breathlessly.

Only silence stirred with their rapid breaths, but only for a moment. Rain began to fall and a cool breeze lifted the white sheer in the open windows. A flash of lightning lit up the darkened room, and then thunder rolled again.

Haley shivered when Shane met her eyes. The faint glow from the outside lamp made the brown in them seem black. And then a new mysterious look crept across his face.

"I have a mind to fall in love with you," he said with a disappointed sigh.

She started to ask him why he sounded discouraged, but he quieted her with his finger to her lips.

Lightning lit the darkness again, a bright flash. Thunder boomed in her ears as if the storm had somehow found its way inside this room. Or maybe it knew the trepidation would make Shane move closer to her.

He chuckled as he held his body to hers, stroking strands of her hair from her face. He slowly pressed his lips to hers, finding a rhythm as she slid her arms around his neck.

Her head spun in excitement and her heart thumped in an undeniable adrenaline rush. She felt him against her stomach, rock solid and completely ready for her.

His chest rose and fell in exhilaration and he groaned as she slid her fingernails gently down to his hips. She massaged bringing her legs around his waist, pulling at him until she couldn't take it anymore.

A gasp of breath came as quick as his hard push. The pain inside her subsided as she began to pull at him wildly. He threw his hips in impatient thrusts, and the wonderful ache made her crave more. She longed for the thrill, for the screams in her breath.

The intensity grew as if they were creating a storm of their own, electrifying their senses. Touching each other in ways only lovers could, kissing passionately, and wanting more than either of them could give.

She threw her arms around his neck and held him tight as his thrusts went deeper and faster. The sensation made her erratic breaths turn to emphatic moans, but he quieted her with another arousing kiss, making her come closer to the breaking point.

He growled as anxiousness lined his sweat-beaded face and heightened veins. And then suddenly, just at the brink of climax, he stopped.

He waited for a moment, catching his breath. She could barely contain the desire for him to continue his hasty push. But when he began again, moving slowly against her, the burning thought dissipated.

Not a word was spoken. He gazed into her eyes, and the meaningful look he gave frightened her. It wasn't the dismissive glance he'd held when they started this thing, but was unusually serious and deep.

He gradually moved his hips, sending a tingling sensation through her body. She felt overpowered by his longing for her, and suddenly felt love, something she knew she didn't deserve. And then the tough woman began to fade into that delicate little shell she so despised.

Why was he doing this to her—making her feel so insecure, so curiously like the damsel in distress? Was she really so sensitive that he could take away all her strength with just a touch?

Afraid he'd see tears welling, she hid her wary glance by turning her head. She closed her eyes, and suddenly his beautiful slow dance stopped.

He stroked her hair away from her eyes and kissed her temple lightly. "Look at me," he whispered.

A sensitive brush of his palm against her cheek made her do as he asked. She desperately wanted to move away from him, calling this beautiful ensemble quits, but she couldn't bring herself to do it.

"I've never seen this look before," he said in a low voice.

She tried to turn her eyes away again, but he wouldn't allow it, holding her face still with his hand. She was sure he could see the tears developing now.

"Did I hurt you?" he asked as he gently wiped a tear from her face.

Haley shook her head. She didn't know what to say, considering her own confusion over why she felt so vulnerable with him.

"You're confused," he guessed aloud and then gave a smirk. "I really shouldn't tell you how I feel about you, Haley, not right at this particular moment."

He shifted his weight slightly as he traced the line of her jaw with his fingers. His movement sent a spark through her as he ran them down her neck and over her nipple. He slid them down her side, tickling her slightly.

"She smiles," he said and then leaned in for a short kiss. "I can't help that I'm falling for you, Haley."

"Don't," she said with a souring look. She tried to push him off, but with his body rigid against her, he wouldn't budge. "This is just sex."

He inspected her face, her sullen eyes. "So you say."

She thought for sure her comment would make him move away from her, but it didn't. Instead he began moving his hips again, slowly and passionately.

"I've never seen fear in your eyes before." He kissed her lightly on the lips. "You're afraid to admit you feel the same way about me."

"You're full of yourself," she moaned.

He thrust a little harder. "I'm not afraid to tell you how I feel."

She grasped his shoulders and pulled close, nestling her face in his neck. She breathed as she wrapped her legs tighter around his waist, trying to hold back long enough for him to start his climax, but she couldn't.

"Then tell me," she said in a moaning breath, holding tight to his neck. "I want to hear you say it."

She could tell by the quickening of his pace that he too couldn't hold on any longer. And as his thrusts intensified, one by one giving her his orgasmic pulse, she cried.

He buried his face in her shoulder, catching his breath. She felt his hands stroking her hair. And when he finally brought his eyes back to hers, his look caught her off-guard. He was frowning.

"I love you, Haley. Maybe a bit too much."

She studied his face. He was completely serious when he said it, but there was still a mysterious look in his eye.

He leaned down and kissed her tenderly on her lips and then moved off of her. For a moment, she thought he'd take her in his arms. She longed for it, especially with the new storm beginning to rage outside. But he moved to the side and lay back, shaking his head as if somehow ashamed.

He let out an irritated sigh. She desperately wanted to get the secrets from him, but he was too reserved. What was he hiding?

"What's wrong?" she asked as she leaned on her side, pulling the sheet around her trembling body.

He flashed an uncertain grin, running his eyes over her pouting lips. "I'm sorry," he apologized as he leaned over and gently kissed her. "I thought this would be easier."

"What would be easier?"

He pondering her question, then shook his head. "It's nothing for you to worry about."

More questions ran through her mind, ones she hadn't thought of before. As he closed his eyes, she lay back and gazed at the ceiling wondering if she even wanted to know the answers. Maybe after this façade was over, they'd part ways never to see each other again, then she'd never have to find out. But curiosity got the better of her.

"You're married," she blurted as she closed her eyes. It was one logical reason why he'd shied away from her after having sex.

"Yes," he answered and her eyes immediately shot open wide.

She turned to look at him, shocked as her heart crept into her throat. And then he laughed. His eyes grew soft as he elbowed her playfully.

"That was a joke, honey."

"Not funny," she replied scowling, but sighed in relief.

"And for your next question, the answer is no. I'm not gay either."

"Then explain. What has your attention?"

"A lot of things," he replied as the seriousness came back to his face. He pulled her in his arms and held her tight. "You're at the top of my list right now."

"What do you mean?" she asked. Her skin rose as he ran his fingers lightly across her back.

"I don't want you here anymore. I don't want him near you, touching you. The way he looks at you makes me sick." His muscles tensed and his jaw tightened. He glared until he couldn't take his anger any longer. He rose from the bed and looked for his clothes.

"So that's what you meant," she said as she watched him slide on his jeans. "When you said you thought this would be easier, you hoped sex would end this fascination we have for each other. But you really did fall in love with me, didn't you?"

He stood before her with his shirt in his hands. Though he looked terribly angry, she could tell he was only pondering her question.

"I thought I'd made myself clear," he said. He put his shirt on and made his way toward the door.

"Where are you going?" she asked as she covered her body with the blanket and leapt to her feet.

"I ..." His voice trailed as she came to stand before him, but he caught his reason. "I'll see you later."

Haley sighed as she watched him disappear in the thick fog. She shut the door and leaned against it. As she scanned the room, her eyes found the clock. It read one AM and as hard as it was to forget the last few hours, she had to get ready for her late night excursion.

Chapter 16

Haley tied her long silky strands back with a small black tie and then checked her form in the mirror. Dressed in a black outfit she looked like a sleek cat, possibly bringing bad luck to anyone crossing her path, especially at this hour. She snapped her matching utility belt lined with a thin rope and her heist tool set, then turned out the lights.

Anticipation grew as she left her room through the back door. She climbed over the deck banister and jumped to the ground. Enveloped in thick fog, she made her way around the main house to the garage. She'd expected the building to be dark, but it was lit brightly and a small group of men stood near the main entrance talking, cigarette smoke permeating the misty air.

Devin's night security was taking a break together, something they'd never do if he were on the property. If she were truly loyal, she'd have a mind to send them back to their posts, reprimanding them for not guarding the place, but this only made her job easier. She crept around the large garage to the back entrance, keeping her eyes on the men. She turned the latch on the door and grinned—unlocked, just as she'd left it. She silently went in and quickly found the black street bike parked inside, keys in the ignition. She kicked the stand and rolled the motorcycle outside and down the grassy hill to the open front gate.

This was much too easy as she rolled it through, ducking beneath the security camera. If she didn't know any better, they had allowed her to sneak out unnoticed as part of a setup. But nobody knew her plans, not even Shane, though she probably should have told him. She also knew he wouldn't have let her do this alone. At least this way she could silently slip in, find the information she needed, and then get out of this entire mess.

After rolling the motorcycle down the road a bit, she hopped on, started the ignition and took off down the city street. And before long, she parked near the docks along the side of an empty parking lot.

She hurried down the tight corridor between warehouses, crouching slightly to avoid being seen over the small crates surrounding her, and careful not to step in puddles from the recent rain. When she reached the outer part of Devin's warehouse, she stopped.

She scanned the area with her night goggles, catching heat from four bodies standing outside the front door of the warehouse. They weren't far away, but it was enough for her to creep around to the side ladder leading to the roof.

She quickly ran from crate to crate, pausing to peek around at the standing bodies. They were oblivious to her presence as she closed the gap between her and the warehouse. Adrenaline pumped through her veins as she grabbed the ladder and climbed just in time for a man to walk beneath her, a gun in his hand.

She waited silently above him, barely breathing and ready to pounce if he saw her. He kept his pace and walked to the front door to join the other men, leaving her to climb.

She peeked over the short cement wall of the roof finding it completely accessible. It was odd that security littered the entire area, but this building, the one with all the goods, remained free. It was almost too good, enough to be suspicious over. But she continued to crawl onto the roof and creep across to the access door on her stomach.

The warehouse was dark and eerily quiet, but thankfully no dogs were patrolling. It seemed everything was working in her favor tonight. Most of the time things went her way, smooth and without a hitch, but this was too strange, too perfect. She had to stay on guard.

She crept down the stairs, scoping the place with her goggles. No movement came from the shadows, and luckily all the crates she'd seen that afternoon were still there. She'd seen Rodriguez punch in the code on the keypad. Hopefully her memory didn't fail her, and with any luck they hadn't changed the number.

After taking one last look around, she hurried to the crate. She carefully punched in the code and the doors unlocked—success.

She hurried inside and closed the door, leaving a slight crack so she could get out when she was done. She took out her small flashlight and looked at the group of boxes before her.

She pulled the latch on one of the boxes and opened it. Her eyes dazzled. Tiny diamonds lined black velvet. She knew Devin had paid a pretty penny for these, if he'd gone legit as he declared.

She opened the next box and found more gems, emeralds, rubies, even gold, but there were no drugs. She wasn't surprised. She'd half-expected everything here to be legitimate, and in a way she was relieved. But now what was she going to do? She couldn't go to Shane without something incriminating. She definitely didn't want this fiasco to keep going, and she knew it would until drugs were found, or the investigation closed. And if that happened, she'd most likely go to jail. Shane had plenty of evidence on her. But would he really do it—could he arrest her and let her rot in prison for the rest of her life?

She went to close the box of diamonds when something strange caught her eye. A tiny hair thread lay across the diamonds, inconspicuously attached to the black velvet. She pinched it with her fingers and gently pulled, lifting the entire box easily from its resting place.

She placed the velvet backing on the table and shined her light inside the hole. At first she couldn't tell what she was seeing, until she reached in and pulled out a clear bag of white powder. Her heart sank when she found more bags stacked together beneath the table.

So it was true. Devin indeed was dealing drugs. She didn't want to believe this, but the evidence was right in front of her. If only she'd left after finding the diamonds, but then all of this would have ended up on the streets. She couldn't let it happen, and suddenly understood Shane's desperation to bring the organization down.

She pulled her cell phone from its pouch on her belt and dialed Shane's number. It was three a.m. and she hoped he'd pick up. But as the phone began to ring, she heard a door slam sending an echo throughout the warehouse.

Shane answered sleepily. "Haley?"

"I'm in the warehouse, Shane," she replied in a whisper. "I found drugs in one of the crates. The number on the lock is five four seven nine zero."

"What the hell are you doing there?" Shane shouted. "Get out of there before you're caught!"

The door to the crate suddenly opened wide and in stepped five burly men. So stunned by the immediate attention, Haley dropped her phone and it slid beneath the table.

They had their hands on her before she could stop them, holding tight to her arms and legs. She struggled to break free as they dragged her out of the crate and carried her into the small office. It took all five men to sit her down in the office chair and tie her to it.

"Make sure it's tight."

Haley glanced at the man speaking from the corner of the room. She couldn't see his face though his voice seemed very familiar. Dressed in blue jeans and a white T-shirt, he stood out among the dark suited men backing against the wall to give him room to approach her.

"We were hoping you wouldn't come, Haley," he said with a sigh. "Well, Devin hoped, anyway. He's got a soft spot for you, though I warned him not to get involved."

The blond man turned around, revealing his identity, and Haley's eyes widened. Flashbacks suddenly swirled through her, from the moment he'd arrived at Chase's house to the day he died on top of that building. She should have realized he was a snake. And now as he stood before her with his confident grin, she knew the truth. Frank Crew was indeed part of the organization.

"Ah," he said as he knelt down in front of her. "You had no idea, did you?" He reached out to stroke her hair, but she jerked her head away.

"You're pathetic," she spat.

He chuckled and then shook his head. "I'm not the one tied up in the chair." He suddenly frowned as he grabbed a handful of her hair and gripped it tight, causing her to cringe. "You stuck your nose where it didn't belong. Do you even understand how disappointed Devin's going to be? I told him you were coming tonight, but he didn't want to believe it."

He let her hair go with a shove and stood straight. He scowled angrily for a moment, but then his face softened into the same inquiring look as before.

"So tell me, did you come because that idiot Shane wanted

you to? Or was it just because you wanted to see for yourself? I understand really, but you know what happens to curious cats, don't you?"

Haley remained quiet at the weak threat. If he wanted to kill her, he'd already done it by now, but he waited on something. Most likely Devin was on his way, and for some reason that frightened her. But she wasn't sure what she was more afraid of, the disappointment he'd feel toward her or the possibility he'd order her death.

"It doesn't matter why you're here anyway," Frank blurted as he gave one of the men along the wall a quick nod. "It just makes my job easier."

The man moved toward her, taking off his leather glove and making a fist. His blank face turned angry as he came to stand before her glaring as he waited patiently for Frank's word.

"What job would that be?" She wondered if this man really meant to hit her. By the way he massaged his large knuckles, she knew her answer.

Frank answered her in a serious voice. "I need to know where they're keeping Chase."

Haley turned her eyes from the man standing before her to Frank's stern face. "You're the cop."

"Haley," Frank retorted, quickly taking hold of the man's arm before he struck her. "They took me off the investigation when I left your group." He crouched before her and flashed a sweet smile, as if his mere looks would get her to talk. "You know where he is. All you have to do is tell me and I'll let you walk out of here. The goods will be gone in a few hours anyway, so I won't tell Devin about this."

Of course he'd think she knew where Chase was. He believed her involvement with Shane would get her back stage privileges to him. But the fact was, she didn't know, and no matter how much she swore it, Frank wouldn't believe her. She braced herself, knowing the next few hours were going to be painful. And by the look on the man's face standing before her, she knew he would enjoy every minute of it.

"I don't know where he is," she said with a smirk. She heard Frank sigh as he stood up. He nodded to the man, then turned his back, obviously afraid to watch.

She saw it coming though she'd planned on shutting her eyes.

The man struck her cheekbone with an open hand, rather than his fist. Though it surprised her, it didn't hurt as bad as she'd expected, but she also knew there would be more to come.

"Come on, Haley," Frank pleaded. "Just give me the information I want. Save yourself from pain."

She turned her face to the side and spit, not only to show her hatred for every person in this room, but because the slap was more painful than she'd thought. Her cheek throbbed, but she still remained emotionless.

She gave a short laugh, causing Frank to turn his glaring eyes on her. "I can't believe Devin would want a sniveling rat like you in his organization when you haven't got the balls to make someone talk."

She glanced at Frank, knowing she'd stoked the fire in his eyes. She wasn't completely sure why she'd provoked him, maybe partly to get what she deserved for being a part of this criminal organization. But more importantly, she meant to stall them until Shane arrived, hopefully bringing the cavalry. And no matter how much they beat on her, even if it meant her death, she knew she'd already won this fight.

On that thought, she felt tremendous pain as the man hit her cheekbone again, this time with a closed fist. Her head twisted to the side from the force and she shut her eyes tight. The high-pitch ring in her ears made her wince.

She took in a deep breath through her nose and then let it out between clenched teeth. Though the ache in her head was almost unbearable, she managed to let out a breathy laugh.

"Beat me all you want, Frank," she said in a painful voice. "I'll never tell you where he is."

He nodded to the man who stood ready to throw another punch. Haley hunched over slightly, trying to endure the pain. She grimaced as she gently ran her tongue along the cut on her lip, tasting the bitterness of blood.

"I know how it feels," Frank said. "I'd really like to keep you from feeling this kind of pain, not to mention ruining your beautiful face."

He paused to look at her for a moment, and then motioned for the man to stop. The man obeyed and dropped back, massaging his knuckles.

"Come on, Haley," Frank said in a quiet voice. "The big guy here can go all day if he has to, though you don't look like you can take much more."

"I ..." she stammered, catching her breath. She managed to open her eyes enough to see the sudden hope in his. And as painful as it was to perform, she smiled. "I'll never tell you where he is."

Tears suddenly welled in her eyes, but they weren't tears from pain. These were tears of triumph. She strained to stay conscious so she could watch the darkly clothed infantry sneak through the warehouse, guns held out before them.

"Why are you smiling?" Frank growled. He grabbed her by the front of her shirt and pulled, causing the chair to screech loudly on the floor. "Tell me, Haley! Where is he?"

"Why do you want to know?" she asked, slurring her words and clenching her teeth. She gazed at him through blurry eyes, hoping to stall him long enough for her savior to get there.

"You know the saying, Haley," he said as he released her. "Once you're in, you're in for life, and there are no exceptions. Our people know too much and I think it's a bad idea, but Devin has a tendency to trust the people he allows in his company. Now look at where it's got him. Chase is ready to testify against him. You've betrayed him by working with the cops. What happened to you, Haley? You were loyal enough to kill for him, but now you want to bite the hand of God?"

"That was before I found out about the drugs," she replied through quick breaths, desperately trying to hang on.

"Drugs, thieves, murderers—they're all criminals, Haley. There's no difference between them, except cocaine turns a bigger profit." He chuckled lightly and then leaned in close to her face. "I can remedy your pain if you'll just tell me where he is."

"And what will happen to me if I tell you?" she asked, knowing what his answer would be.

"That depends on you," he said as he opened the top drawer of the desk. He pulled out a gun and inspected its dark metal finish as he continued. "I'm tired of these games, Haley. It's time you talked. I would really rather not kill you. But if I have to, I will."

"Frank," she said with effort. "You might as well pull the trigger now. If you don't, when I get out of here ..." she paused to show him the seriousness in her eyes. "I'm coming to find you."

Frank immediately raised his arm, and using the butt of the gun hit her across the face. She cried out in agony just as many other voices flooded her ears, including one tenor she desperately prayed to hear again.

Profanities along with demands for everyone to get down on the floor set loose in the small office. Although she couldn't see through her blinding pain, she knew her assailants obeyed the demands, at least until someone grabbed her by the throat.

The pain was excruciating as she opened her blurry eyes. Blood mixed with her tears, but she could make out Shane's figure standing before her, gun pointed just above her right shoulder.

"Let her go, Frank," Shane warned, unflinching.

"No," Frank said, his breath erratic as he frantically untied Haley from the chair. He held the gun to her head as he forced her up to her feet. "Get back or your precious gem dies!"

Haley saw Shane back away slowly, followed by the other cops, but their guns remained pointed forward. Frank shoved her toward the door leaving his grip tight around her arm.

She could easily get out of this if she weren't so weak. Drifting in and out of consciousness, she let him lead her out into the warehouse and back toward the exit.

"Just shoot him," she pleaded, cringing at the sound of her own voice. It hurt to speak making her buckle over slightly.

"Shut up," Frank demanded through clenched teeth, keeping his hold on her as he backed her outside. He turned just in time to see a display of policemen waiting for him.

He pressed the gun to Haley's skull and scanned the lineup. As Shane and his team fled out the front door, Frank found the black Spider parked on the side of the warehouse.

"Where're your keys?" He shook her slightly as he inched closer to the car.

Haley refused to answer. She'd never give in to him, even if it meant he'd fire a bullet into her brain. If she was going to die, she'd go down fighting. And as if the very idea gave her strength, she began to struggle.

It hurt like hell, but she managed to toss her head back into his nose. She fell hard to her knees disoriented but aware enough to hear the spray of gunfire break out.

Then she fell to the ground, her face becoming numb as a new pain developed in her side. And when she felt warm, gentle hands envelop hers, and her savior's voice call her name, everything went black.

Chapter 17

Haley opened her eyes to blinding light. The consistent beep from a machine, like a large truck backing in the distance, grew louder as she became more awake.

Able to somewhat focus, she found herself lying in a room, walls painted light blue maybe to make the tenant feel a little better. Machines were turned on beside the bed, causing a much more distinct sound than when she'd first awoken. She could hear the drip of the fluid in the bag connected to the needle in her arm. And it was then she realized where she was—a hospital.

She remembered most of what happened though she'd been almost unconscious. The beating she'd taken to prove to a bad cop just where her loyalty lay was immensely painful, but well worth it, she hoped. It'd given Shane enough time to get there with his team, but after that her memory was vague.

She pulled herself up in the bed, but pain shot through her side. She winced and groaned just as the door to her room opened and someone came in holding a large display of colorful flowers.

"It's about time you woke up," Shane said as he set the large bouquet down on the bedside table. He made his way to her side and inspected her face, frowning. "How are you feeling?"

She cleared her throat and in a strained voice answered, "Like hell."

He swiped a lock of her hair over her ear. "You look like it, too."

"That's a nice way to thank the person who gave you the bust of the century."

"Don't joke about it. You put yourself on the line." He shook his head and carefully sat down on the edge of the bed. "You almost got yourself killed."

"You caught Devin, didn't you?" she asked. "And Frank," she paused for a second, "what happened to him?"

"Devin's always been one step ahead of us. He disappeared. Seems the warehouses aren't even in his name. They're owned by the shipping company. They leased it out to someone without doing a background check. If they had, they would have learned the person renting it used a name from the obituaries."

"But the crates," Haley said, trying to sit up, rather upset over this news. She tried to ignore the pain, but it was too much. She hunched over holding her side.

Shane took hold of her shoulders to straighten her out. He gently helped her lay back on the bed and pushed the button for the nurse when he saw blood soaking through her bandage. "You were shot, Haley. So just take it easy."

A gray-haired nurse walked in the room and immediately checked her bandage. "You need to stop moving around, young lady," she said as she peeled off the tape and removed the gauze. "Your stitches look okay, but you need to heal before trying to get up. Might as well get comfortable, you're going to be here for a few more days."

"I have nowhere to go anyway," Haley replied as she closed her swollen eyes.

The nurse finished bandaging her wound, shut off the monitor, ending the irritating beep, and then left with a warning to Shane.

"Don't over-stimulate the patient or I'm going to kick you out myself. She needs her rest," the nurse said.

He promised before she shut the door and left them alone in the now quiet room.

"You never answered me," Haley reminded him without opening her eyes. "What happened to Frank?"

"He fired his gun. We didn't have any other choice but to take him down."

Haley opened her eyes. "Oh," she said in a whisper, but it was all she could say about it. She'd taken the blame for Frank's previous stunt, and he didn't deserve sympathy this time, though it slowly came. In a way she understood his reason for protecting Devin. The organization sucked in weak individuals and made it look like heaven, as long as they stayed loyal. Frank probably earned a great deal of money, and possibly even a little power-trip, something she was sure he never received from the police force.

"It's not your fault," Shane said as he took his place at the edge of the bed. He stroked her head gently. "I wish you would have told me what your plans were though. I could have saved you from this."

"The crates in the warehouse," she said, ignoring his comment. She carefully sat up this time.

"We confiscated them. Devin's a slippery bastard. He knows how to cover his tracks, but I think we're close to finding him."

"I can help you. And then I'll testify against him right along with Chase."

"No, Haley," Shane said. "You've already done enough."

"Don't be ridiculous. You have enough evidence to arrest him and put him away for the rest of his life. I have information on every heist he's ordered us to do. I can give you locations, dates, times, even what was stolen. All you have to do is check your theft reports. They'll coincide."

She cringed in pain, but this time it was her head. It ached in a terrible way. She lay back and concentrated on breathing to release the tension.

"You'd be incriminating not only Devin, but the rest of your group too, including yourself. Chase already agreed to take a fall for you. He made me promise to keep you out of jail, but I couldn't make any deals for the others."

She thought about it for a moment. "Then let me take the fall for them."

"Just shut up and rest now. Try not to worry about anything. It's taken care of." He stood up preparing to leave. The look he gave her was unusual, but she dismissed it as worry.

"Stay with me," she said as she reached for his hand and he met her half way. He sat back down on the bed and softly stroked her fingers between his.

"I'm sorry I left you the other night," he said. "I guess I was a bit of a jerk. If I hadn't left, you wouldn't be here right now, looking like this."

Haley watched him as he twisted his lips to the side. This was a new light, a sensitive side of him he didn't show often.

"Why, Shane Sin," she replied with a slight smile, ignoring the pain that came with it. "Are you apologizing to me?"

"I suppose I am," he said, relaxing his face. "And by the way, Shane Sin's my undercover name."

Though it hurt, she couldn't help but laugh. "I know."

"Of course you do," he replied curiously. "I suppose Haley's your cover."

"I think I'm the only one in the group that actually used my real name. It's only because I never had family to protect, at least none I knew of. Chase was the closest thing I had." She looked away, careful not to show how much she really wanted to know. "So what is your real name? Or is it still a secret?"

"You can still call me Shane. Last name isn't Sin, it's Hawke."

"Shane Hawke," she said as she placed her hand on her stomach. She got a strange look on her face as a gurgling sound interrupted their conversation.

"Hungry?" he asked. Before she could answer, he stood up, leaned over and kissed her lightly on the forehead. "I'll get you something to eat."

He turned to leave, but she caught him by the hand and stopped him. And when he turned around, he saw tears glittering in her swollen eyes.

"Thank you," she said, her voice breaking into a whisper. "If you hadn't come..."

"No worries," he interrupted, squeezing her hand. He raised it to his lips and kissed her palm, pausing to hold it against his face. And then he gently released it to her side. "I'll be right back."

Her eyes burned so she shut them. A sudden tiredness won over her hunger and she drifted off into a light slumber, feeling like she hadn't slept in months. She couldn't remember the last time she'd dreamt, though she'd never really cared for dreams. They were worthless images, unrealistic and impossible. But now, as Shane entered her mind—his loving arms around her, she wanted to sleep. He took away her pain as he carried her through soft white clouds.

Haley heard a short clicking sound. She opened her eyes to find a man dressed in a doctor's overcoat standing beside her, pointing a gun in her face. He waved it, motioning her to get up and into the wheelchair sitting before him.

"Not a word or I'll kill you," he said. "Just get in the chair."

"I can't," she replied, emphasizing the IV.

The man impatiently pulled the needle from her vein causing her to let out a painful shout. He lifted her from the bed, set her down in the wheelchair, and wheeled her out the door.

The pain in her side wasn't so bad, but the dizziness in her aching head was excruciating. She desperately wanted to scream, but she couldn't find her voice, not until she saw Shane walking from the other end of the hall carrying a tray of food.

"Shane!" she screamed.

He sprinted toward them as the man behind her growled and fled from the chair, disappearing through the stairway door just as Shane reached her.

"You alright?" he asked in a frantic voice, handing her the tray without completely stopping.

"Fine," she said as she watched him pull his gun. He headed toward the stairwell door, and disappeared after her assailant.

She breathed out a sigh of relief when she felt the wheelchair turn back toward her room. The wound in her side hadn't ripped opened, but the warming sensation on her skin let her know she was bleeding again.

"Wait," she said in a strangled voice as they wheeled past her room. She turned to find a woman in a nurse's uniform wearing a white mask over her face, hiding her identity. Nobody seemed to notice she didn't belong, but by her silence, and her refusal to go back, Haley knew. And suddenly she was aware that the first attempt to abduct her was nothing more than a diversion.

"I have a gun aimed at you," the nurse said, seeing the panic in Haley's eyes. "One word and nothing would give me more pleasure than to put a bullet in your head."

That voice. It sounded so familiar though the woman tried to disguise it. And when they got on the elevator, Haley looked closer.

Her hair was thick and brown, cut over her ears. But her eyes, glaring and dazzling, gave her away.

"I've often wondered what happened to you, Sara," Haley said in a calm voice. She watched the numbers above the elevator door rise, and realized they were heading toward the roof.

"Shut up, Haley," Sara snapped. "I'm supposed to deliver you in one piece."

Haley couldn't help but laugh a little, as much as the pain would let her. It wasn't condescending at all, but she knew Sara would take it as such.

"What happened to us, Sara?" Haley continued. "We used to be friends."

"That was before you betrayed us," Sara said. "Devin told me everything. I used to look up to you. Smart, beautiful, lethal, you had all the attributes I wanted. I envied you then." She let out a condescending laugh. "Now look at you. Devin's going to make you pay for what you tried to do to the company."

"He won't."

"He's already got plans for you, precious. If you think Frank did a number on you, just wait. And your sexy cop won't be able to do anything to save you," Sara said.

The elevator reached the top floor and Sara wheeled her out. She hurried down the hallway to the stairs and opened the door.

"You have to walk now," Sara said as she grabbed Haley's arm and shoved her out of the wheelchair, making her land on the stairs hard.

The pain was excruciating as she crept up the last short flight of stairs, Sara holding tight to her arm. She clutched her side and felt the stickiness of blood drenching her hand, knowing there was nothing she could do but go with her.

Haley heard angry voices below them as Sara opened the door to the roof. She leaned over the railing and looked down, just in time to catch Shane glancing at her.

"Shane!" she yelled but was cut off by Sara's gripping hands.

She was shoved out onto the windy roof where other hands grabbed her and carried her to a waiting helicopter, whirring loudly ready to whisk her away. Her hair whipped around her face as they pulled her through the door and forced her into a seat.

The sound of the propellers increased as they lifted into the sky, leaving the hospital behind. She saw Shane aiming his gun as he moved toward them, desperately wanting to fire but unable for fear he might hit her. And then she saw him fall to his knees, lower his gun, and watch her fly away.

Chapter 18

The inside of Dragon used to be comforting. Haley had often closed her eyes and listened to its growl as it carried her and her team across the sky, landing on their target building or in the middle of a field. And as if welcoming them home with open arms, it was always waiting for them when their job was done, a beautiful sight. Then they'd climb in and leave their worries behind, knowing they'd pulled off their job perfectly.

This time it felt like the enemy, growling loudly against her aching head. It despised her just as much as Sara did, as if somehow she'd programmed it to do so. She couldn't blame either of them, understanding the loyalty they felt to their master. She'd felt it too, though it seemed so long ago.

It was revolting to follow such a man as Devin. He had the charm of a true gentleman, but deep down he was pathetic, hiding behind the skirt of his father's company, and hiding behind innocent people who'd already lived their life and had fallen in God's grace. But his despicable choices had been well played, earning his freedom, though that would change now.

With her knowledge of his dealing, there was no doubt she'd testify against him. He believed himself invincible, a demanding demeanor. A barrier drawn around his territory would only make him want to break it down and go further, testing what his boundaries really are, and breaking them as well.

This was exactly the case with her. He wanted her. And regardless of her disloyalty to him, he'd never give up until he had her, or killed her. And unfortunately, she'd never give in to him, making the answer simple.

They landed in the backyard at his mansion on the coast. They forced her out of the helicopter and across the yard to the back patio of the house. Devin, along with several dozen of his bodyguards, stood on the top steps waiting for her. His stare was blank, expressionless as they led her up the short steps to meet him, but when he saw blood staining her clothes, his face softened.

As the helicopter wound down, Devin took her arm and led her into the house. He helped her sit down on the couch, and his face suddenly grew angry.

"Damn Frank and his antics!" he shouted, causing everyone in the room to jump. "Get me some gauze and tape, and a fresh change of clothes for her," he ordered his nearest guard, and the man immediately set out to find what he wanted. "I'm so sorry, Haley." He returned his attention to her. "Frank wasn't supposed to go this far."

"Frank's dead," Haley replied, rather shocked by his ignorant approach with her, especially after he'd sent out more of his thugs to retrieve her from the hospital.

"I heard," he insisted. "You must think I'm a monster. But please, let me explain."

She could spit on him for being a coward, not wanting to take the blame for what happened to her, but she closed her eyes and waited for his excuse. Of course, it didn't really matter anyway. She wouldn't believe him.

"Frank told me about your involvement with the police just after Chase was … killed," he said as he glanced down at her side. "We really need to change your bandage."

Haley knocked his hand away when he reached for her. His guards suddenly stepped forward, but he quickly put his hand up to stop their advance.

"It's fine," he snapped. He stood up as one of his guards brought in the gauze and tape and a pullover short sleeve dress, and handed it to Haley. "Everyone out," he ordered.

At first none of them moved, afraid to leave him alone in the room with her. But when he flashed an impatient scowl, they piled out onto the porch.

Devin closed the door behind them and then sighed when he turned around. "You realize how much you've cost my company," he said as he sat down in the chair beside her. He rested his ankle on his knee and watched her remove the old gauze and redress it.

"You did it to yourself," Haley said, almost breathless in pain.

"If you had only left the legacy your father left you alone. You got greedy, Devin."

"Everyone is entitled to seek more, especially when their usual income is beginning to diminish. The auctions were bringing in less fortune and more irritation. Not to mention finding jewels to steal was becoming difficult."

"What happened to going legitimate?" Haley retorted as she slid the blue dress on.

"I have gone straight," he replied in earnest. "The jewels you found are not stolen."

"It's just a front for your drug operation." She gazed at him solemnly. "Why, Devin? Why did you go there?"

He tossed her a confused, but serious glance. "There's ten times more money in one shipment of cocaine than there is in selling a year's worth of jewelry. Times are hard for people and they're not buying materialistic things. Cocaine is a seller, however. It's like food for the weary, a high to end the pain of the past and a way to face the future with ambiguous eyes. Who wants to face a future of despair? I intend to help these people through troubled times. And if that means I make a little money in return, I believe it's worth it."

"You're a sick man if you believe you're helping society," Haley said seeing him in a completely new way. "You're nothing but a greedy, self-righteous bastard."

"Call me what you will," he said. "I'm still rich and quite in control of this situation."

"What do you mean?" Haley asked. Her skin prickled when she saw him grin.

"You remember Rodriguez," he insisted, ignoring her question. "He didn't know how to manage his inherited cartel, so I bought him out, so-to-speak. Now the money is flowing in. My only regret is that I have to leave this place behind and go live in Mexico. Not such a bad deal really, it's a rather beautiful place near the beach. The water is so blue it almost looks as if the sky never ends. You'll love it."

She rose up in the couch, cringing from the pain. "What do you want with me?"

"You should know I never forgive traitors." Then he sighed and leaned forward, giving her his full attention. "But I'm willing to make an exception for you, Beautiful. On one condition, of course," he added.

"And what's that?"

"I believe it's rather agreeable."

One of the guards walked into the room and cleared his throat. "Sir," he said, his voice trembling slightly. "The ship's reached international waters. We need to go."

"Yes, I'm aware," Devin replied impatiently. Without taking his eyes off Haley, he stood up. "Fire up the engine, we'll be there in a moment."

We—that meant he was planning on taking her with him. She wasn't about to go anywhere. She'd fight him with all her strength, even if it meant all the pain she could endure.

"Come with me, not as a member of my organization, but as my wife. I'll give you everything you desire—wealth, power, my heart. I'll love you forever, if you allow me to."

Nausea crept to the back of her throat at even the thought of it. "You know nothing of my desires. I'm not going anywhere with you," she hissed angrily and quickly stood up.

Her sudden movement caused Devin to stumble back and yell for his bodyguards. Four large men rushed into the room, guns held before them. But they were no match for Haley's quick reflexes as one by one, they went down before they had any clue what was happening.

Adrenaline pumped through her, limiting the pain as she turned to deal with Devin, but he'd already escaped to the deck. She took off after him as he ran across the lawn to the helicopter, where Sara sat waiting to take off. There was no way in hell she'd allow them to get away, not this time.

As the helicopter lifted off the ground, she grabbed hold of the skid. She pulled her body up, quickly opened the door, and struck Sara in the face, rendering her useless at the controls. The helicopter began to spin.

Haley hopped inside just as the chopper landed roughly back on the ground, turning on its side. The propellers bent and cracked, sending sparks flying through the cabin when they punctured the roof, just nearly missing her, but unfortunately grabbing hold of Sara.

Haley lay on the floor, her head swimming in dizziness as the wreckage finally came still. Someone lifted her out of the burning helicopter and carried her across the yard to the house. He sat her down in the chair and immediately tied her up before she could regain her composure.

"The plan has changed, but we need her alive. She's ransom now," Devin spoke to someone in the room, and her eyes adjusted on a dark figure in the corner.

As Devin left, she watched the figure roll a silver ball over his fingers as if he were a performer at a circus. His large bifocal glasses reflected the light from the room, a smirk playing on his lips. Michael.

He quickly threw the ball onto her lap, causing her to flinch. She panicked as she watched a strange blue mist rise from it, and its odd-scented smoke billowed around her.

She desperately tried to move, but her legs wouldn't allow it. The sensation was familiar, like the paralyzing grip Shane used on her before, but she couldn't feel anything this time.

"Why are you doing this?" She tried not to panic, but he only walked up the steps and left the room, leaving her helpless, and paralyzed from the waist down.

Chapter 19

It seemed like she'd sat in the same chair for weeks, but she knew only about forty minutes went by. And it had only been a few minutes since Devin had thrown a cover over her eyes and dressed her in some sort of uncomfortable cloth vest. And though there was a small amount of light through the dark fibers, she couldn't see where he'd gone.

She struggled to remove the rope around her wrists, but it wouldn't budge. Her ankles were chafed from the same kind of burn, and her waist was tied to the chair, but she would never give up. She twisted in her seat, hoping to find a way to get out of this without dislocating her shoulders, but it seemed inevitable.

She breathed in deep, ready to endure the pain as she began to raise her arms behind her and over her head. Her muscles tightened in her neck as she clenched her teeth and popped one shoulder out of its socket.

Tears sprung to her eyes and she let out an agonizing shout, but she refused to give in. "One more," she whispered to herself, wishing to God she had jumped from the helicopter instead of inside it.

Gritting her teeth, she pulled her other shoulder around ready to suffer more pain when she heard a magnificent but urgent shout for her to stop. His footsteps quickly moved toward her, and then the dark bag came off her head. She was ever so glad to find those beautiful muddy eyes before her.

"Shane," she said frantically. "My arm …" her voice trailed as he immediately took hold of it and shoved it back into place. "Get me out of here," she groaned in an agonizing breath.

He gently touched her face and shook his head in frustration. "I can't Haley," he said through clenched teeth. "You're wired."

"What do you mean?"

It was then she remembered the vest they put on just moments before. The heaviness against her chest suddenly came about causing the pressure on her wound to grow.

The sudden scene of the women tied in the crate spun in her mind. The inevitable demise from the bombs strapped to their chest was about to become her untimely ending as she found several blocks of C4 wired to a timer. It ticked down on a black box in bold green letters, and the numbers were running low.

"Five minutes, Shane," she whispered.

"The bomb squad will be here in no time," he said, attempting a smile that came out a grimace. "Don't worry. I'll get you out of here."

"Where's Devin?" she asked, trying to keep her mind off her death sentence.

"He called me a little while ago giving me instructions to bring Chase here. He threatened to kill you if I didn't deliver him."

"Oh no, please tell me you didn't trade Chase for me."

He shook his head. "I didn't know, Haley. I didn't know he'd do this."

"Shane," she said. "As long as Chase is safe, it's okay."

He arched his brow. "You're unbelievable."

"I know where he's going," she whispered, tugging at the rope bound around her sore wrists.

"Let's worry about getting you safely out of here first," he said as he took a closer look at the bomb.

"There's not enough time to save us both," she said. "Just go, save yourself!"

"I'll figure this out," he replied. "I worked with a guy on the bomb squad once. He showed me a few things."

"But this is Michael's handiwork," she whispered. "Even if you get it disconnected ..."

"Shut up, Haley," he said. "I'm trying to concentrate."

"Just please, go," she said struggling to fight back tears. "Devin has a ship waiting for him in international waters. If you leave now, maybe you can get to him before he reaches the docks. He'll take the side streets. Go, before he gets away."

"I'm not leaving you." He inspected the wires. "Did you know I cleaned my house?" he asked, completely changing his tone with the subject as he took out his pocket knife. His breath came fast as if he'd sprinted a mile in a race. "I've been meaning to get the car engine off my dining table for several years, but never had a reason until now. I plan on cooking you dinner once this is over. And did you know I found a detached garage in my backyard? I could've been working there this entire time."

His attempt to make her relax fell flat as strong emotions took over her fear. She lost her breath as if a fist suddenly hit her in the gut knocking the wind from her. The terrible pains in her chest seemed to crush her as if trying to squeeze every built up emotion she'd buried inside to the surface.

"We're going to die," she said, gasping for air as the clock hit one minute. She held her emotions back with all her strength. And when she finally looked into his eyes, the answer to what really caused the pain hit her hard and fast—she was desperately in love with him.

"You cleaned your house," she said. Of all things to surprise her, especially at a moment like this, this ranked up there with the best.

"Now wait," he said, taken back by her sudden change of demeanor. "Don't look at me that way. I'm not the one who cleaned, though I should let you go on believing that lie." He cleared his throat, glancing at her as if he were the one being interrogated, and he was terribly guilty. "I do have a maid—err … a sister who helps me on occasion."

"You have a sister?" Haley asked surprised.

"Yes, but please don't tell her I called her a maid. She'd have me killed for sure."

The panic of the moment hung thick in the air, but she was happy staring into the most beautiful eyes she'd ever seen, though they mirrored her fear. She knew then what he was about to do. And with only seconds left, it was the only thing he could do.

"I love you, Shane," she blurted as he held the edge of the knife against the green wire.

He glanced at her briefly. "Now you tell me."

Haley closed her eyes and waited for him to break the wire. She heard the snap and then a gasping breath from Shane. Her eyes opened to a cloud of red mist as Shane held his breath and began working frantically on the ropes.

He freed her from the bomb, lifted her up into his arms, and carried her outside on the deck. Without stopping, he set her down on her feet, and took her by the hand. And as they ran like hell, the C4 exploded.

It sent them flying out onto the lawn followed by a roll of fire and smoke. A thunderous boom echoed around them causing the glass to blow from the windows and sending the wrecked helicopter off the cliff.

Haley landed hard with Shane right beside her. Pieces of metal fell around them and shards of glass dropped, glittering like diamonds across the green yard.

When the debris finally came still, she crawled to Shane who lay on his stomach with his eyes closed. "You okay?" she asked, completely out of breath as she ran her fingers through his hair.

He opened his eyes and groaned. "I'm good—you?" he replied in an exhausted breath.

She turned over on her back and breathed a sigh. "I feel like hell."

He sat up and hovered over her, inspecting her face for any new wounds. He ran his hand across her temple, swiping her hair from her fatigued face, and then he grinned.

"But you look so damn beautiful," he said, and then leaned down and kissed her on the lips.

He leapt to his feet and then pulled her up to hers. She cringed, holding her side as he led her around the burning house.

"I have to go, Haley. He couldn't have gone far at this time of day. Listen," he said as he helped her across the courtyard where his car was parked amidst a dozen police cars. "Go back to the hospital. I'll meet you there when this is over."

"I will not," she argued.

"Don't be stubborn. I'll make sure you're protected."

"I don't need protected," she said as she buckled over slightly. She held her breath for a moment. "I'm going with you."

"No, you're not," he said and folded his arms over his chest. "You're going to do what I tell you to do. It's for your own good."

"I owe him."

"You're in no shape for revenge," he replied.

"Shane—"

"I'll call you as soon as he's in custody," he insisted as he left her standing near the front of the car. "I promise this will all be over by the end of the day."

She knew she was too weak to be of any help and would probably end up getting herself killed, but still, she felt it her duty to bring Devin down. And there was no way in hell she'd allow it to happen without her.

She quickly hopped into Shane's car, just as he started the engine. She reached over and locked the door when he leaned over and tried the latch, attempting to kick her out.

"What do you think you're doing?"

"I'm going with you."

"Get out of the car, Haley! It's too dangerous."

"I'm not getting out," she said as she buckled her seatbelt. "You better drive before he gets away. I'd say he has a good twelve minutes on us."

While he shifted the car into gear and sped off down the driveway, he announced his pursuit over the scanner—Devin was heading to the docks. Tires screeched as he pulled out onto the highway and accelerated down the short strip of road.

"You could have been killed ... again. I can't let you risk your life anymore."

"Speak for yourself," she retorted as she watched a line of fire trucks and ambulances pass them heading toward the now blazing mansion behind them. "You've risked everything for me. So I've made this my fight. And I'm going to win."

"Your fight?" he asked. The seriousness in her face made him belt out a single laugh. "You've had a hard enough time as it is. For once give up the war and lean on someone."

"And just who am I going to lean on?"

"Me, of course." He was rather shocked she had to ask such a ridiculous question. "But you're too stubborn to listen to me."

"When this is over, just put me in prison with the others."

"I'm not throwing you in jail with a bunch of criminals. You don't belong there, so quit saying that."

"Then where exactly do I belong?" She knew his answer, and before he could tell her she belonged with him, she gave him her reply. "I am a criminal Shane. I'll face up to my crimes just like everyone else."

"Always the tough girl."

"Always," she interrupted. "Just promise you won't wait for me. You have a lot to offer someone who's good and just. You deserve better than me."

"Give me a break," he replied as they pulled down a side street. "Like I said—you're not doing time. So you might as well give up and say you belong with me, because you're not winning that war."

It was just like a dream, a bad one maybe, but when Haley saw Devin's familiar red sports car up ahead, she immediately cast a defiant smile. "There he is," she said, divulging a plan in her mind of what tortuous things she'd do to him once she had him in her grasp.

Shane had already noticed Devin's license plate and sped up, weaving around traffic. He seemed slightly perturbed over her ignoring his comment, but made no attempt to argue as he quickly caught up to Devin's car, tailing it close.

He pulled a police light from beneath his seat and carefully stuck it on the roof. "Tighten your seatbelt," he told her as Devin's car quickly sped up. "He's running, of course. The bad guys always run."

Haley did as she was told, listening as Shane told dispatch about the pursuit, calling off Devin's license plate in a series of names and numbers. A thrill overpowered her, an adrenaline rush she'd never experienced before as they sped around cars and through alleys she swore they'd never fit through. It gave her an irrepressible chill, fearing he'd put one small scrape on the perfect blue paint of his beloved car, but he drove like a pro.

She remembered him telling her that she was his first love, but she knew better now. He carried the slightest grin as he drove, tires screeching, pushing the engine to its maximum capacity as he chased the bad guy down. But the ability to outdrive the most ruthless crime lord around wasn't what made him radiate magnificently. It wasn't her either, though she believed she took a close second, and for that she was truly pleased.

No, this man's first love wasn't a woman, and it wasn't a souped-up muscle car. His first love was all about being a cop, sworn to protect and serve. Having saved her from being beaten to death and blown to pieces, he obviously performed well above any set guidelines.

She suddenly looked at him with the utmost adoration. She

loved him; there was no doubt in her mind now. And though she'd voiced it before, believing it her last confession, she desperately wanted to tell him just how much she meant it.

Her thoughts were suddenly jostled as the car hit air coming over a steep hill. The unbelievable sensation of flying electrified her in such an orgasmic way that she lost her breath in an emphasized laugh. Chills spread through her, causing each hair on her body to stand until the car landed hard on the pavement.

The front axel bent and broke as Shane slammed on the brakes. The crash of metal and screeching tires pierced Haley's ears until they finally came to a halt just before smashing into a parked car on the curb.

Shane was out of the car in a flash, his gun drawn and pointed forward, disregarding that his car lay in pieces around him. Haley opened her door.

"Get back in," he demanded without a glance. "You better call for an ambulance."

Haley could barely concentrate on searching for a cell phone as she caught the sight in front of her. With her mouth agape, she watched as Shane neared the wreckage of Devin's car. By the looks of it, he'd lost control, ultimately rolling it down the length of the road until it finally landed on its top in a heap of twisted metal.

Her skin rose again as she frantically looked for Shane's phone. She searched in the glove compartment, on the floor, and in the crease between the padding of the seat, but she couldn't find it. The only thing she found was a loaded silver semi-automatic and she was absolutely prepared to use it.

The dispatcher's voice came across the radio, and she quickly picked it up. She pressed the button on the side and breathed a nervous sigh.

"Hello," she said, feeling rather ridiculous for saying it. But the voice came back with the same greeting, bringing back her confidence. "We need an ambulance at an accident on Leland and Mello Street. It involves Devin Yoshino."

Haley glanced up to watch Shane move along the side of Devin's car. He was ready for anything as he leaned around the frame of the door and peered inside, but he wasn't prepared to find it empty.

He crouched and scanned the area, finding small droplets of blood that led up to the sidewalk. He followed the trail, pausing to glance around him.

Haley scanned the parked cars, searching for him. She knew he had to be badly injured, but a snake like him could easily strike from the shadows when the moment was right. It was then she found him, leaning up against one of the cars with a gun in his hands, and he was just behind hane.

Sirens sounded off in the distance. The cavalry was on its way, but she knew they'd be too late. She left the car, unsheathed the gun and made her way toward the parked cars.

"Drop the gun, Devin!" she shouted just as he took aim at Shane's back.

"You drop your gun," Devin said in a choked breath. "I will shoot him."

"It's over, Devin," Haley said. "Just give yourself up. You know I'll pull the trigger."

"And you know I'll pull mine," he replied and then focused on Shane. "Drop your gun and turn around."

Shane slowly turned holding his hands up enough to show he was giving in. He eyed Haley sharply as if reprimanding her for getting out of the car when he told her not to, but then turned his attention to Devin.

"Put the gun down, Haley, and step over beside your boyfriend," he demanded through clenched teeth. "I'm taking your car."

"My car..." Shane whispered as he finally caught sight of the damaged front-end. He cleared his throat and then focused again on Devin. "You should give up now."

"Don't tell me what I should do!" Devin shouted as he backed toward the car. "You have two seconds to move or I'll shoot."

Though still sore from the tribulations over the past week, she found the strength to quickly grab Devin by the hand and knock the gun from his grasp before he pulled the trigger. The gun went spiraling to the ground. He reached to recover it, but Haley knocked him to the side with her foot.

She aimed her gun at him and stood, ready to pull the trigger. So many times she'd been in situations where she had to draw her gun, but never did she lose her cool. Never did she allow anyone the chance to fight back. But for some reason as she stood holding the gun at her former boss—a giant in the criminal community, she trembled.

"I should kill you," she hissed.

Shane watched as she fought with her inner demon, taking steps toward the defenseless man, aiming her gun like she meant to shoot. Her finger squeezed the trigger slightly, but then she'd let off knowing it'd be wrong to go through with it. This happened several times, and he knew then she desperately needed intervention.

"Haley," Shane said, careful not to startle her into turning the gun on him. "It's okay; you can put the gun down."

He moved toward her, but she turned her angry eyes on him. "Stay back!" she yelled, ignoring the dozen police cars coming to a screeching halt near the wrecked car. "He doesn't deserve to live."

Seeing cops quickly surrounding the area, there was no place Devin could run. Shane sheathed his gun and walked slowly toward her hoping he'd get to her in time before she shot the wounded man on the ground. And by the way her body trembled when he touched her he knew how hard she struggled.

"You're not a killer," Shane said as he placed his hand over hers. He applied pressure, coaxing her to lower the weapon.

She clenched her teeth and leaned on him. He comforted her, and slowly the anger began to fade. It helped to look at something else besides the low-life on the ground, and found her focus on the uniformed cops making their way toward them.

"I won't go to jail," Devin said, and Haley's eyes came back to him. He grabbed the gun on the ground, took aim at Shane, and pulled the trigger.

Haley shoved Shane out of the path of the bullet just in time for it to miss the back of his head. It whizzed past her, skimming her cheek, leaving the slightest mark with a trace of blood. She reflexively lifted her gun and squeezed the trigger before he shot again.

Shane immediately went to him. He pulled the gun from his hand without any resistance, and knew the man was dead.

Haley stood shocked at what she'd done. For some reason she thought killing him would bring her satisfaction, but it did nothing short of cause her remorse.

"I'm sorry," she whispered as she dropped her gun to the ground.

"Don't be sorry," Shane said as he made his way to her. "You saved my life, Haley. If you hadn't pushed me out of the way ..."

"I killed him."

Shane led her away from the scene as the other cops took over. He leaned her up against his broken car and caressed her arms.

"You almost took a bullet for me," he said. "Everyone here saw how courageous and strong you are."

"I'm weak," she argued. "I'm no better than him."

"No," he said leaning his forehead against hers. "You could never be like him. You're good, Haley." He took her face in his hands and then let out a relieved breath. "Maybe you have a small, very miniscule problem with authority, but I think I can change that."

It wasn't exactly the best time to make jokes, but when he kissed her, the remorse faded. And in a serious voice, he whispered in her ear reassuring words. "Everything will be okay. I'll protect you. I'll love you forever. So what do you say we fly to Reno and get hitched?"

He'd tickled her ear with his whispers, but these words made her lean back and look him in the eye. He was completely serious, unflinching, unyielding, and terribly attractive as he stared her down. This was a complex look, one she'd never seen before.

Haley shivered in a pure adrenaline rush. "I thought you were arresting me."

He kissed her lightly on the lips and then tapped the handcuffs on his belt. "You have the right to remain silent." His eyes fixed on her trembling lips, the undeniable seriousness in her gaze and then gave a defeated sigh. "You really want to go to jail? Hell, Haley, we can play cops and robbers all day long if you want, but when you get serious enough to listen to what I'm saying, then give me a call."

She watched in awe as he walked to the front of the car and inspected the terrible damage. He frowned, shaking his head as he pulled out his cell phone and sat down in the passenger side. He pulled the papers from the glove compartment and found his insurance card, cursing under his breath.

This was ridiculous, Haley thought as she glanced around at the cops. A man took digital pictures of the body lying on the ground, the one she put there. So why was she still standing here? They were supposed to arrest her for the crimes she'd committed.

She looked at Shane and it suddenly dawned on her. She wouldn't go to jail because of him. She'd remain free because she'd found her true calling in life, and that was being with him.

He stood up, and she walked to him. "Okay then, what did you have in mind?" she asked.

He gently palmed her cheek with an adoring grin. And then her heart leapt as he took her by the hand. "I was going to ask you before, but obviously we were busy." He thought for a moment. "Then maybe I should ask you tonight at home."

"Home?" she said, catching herself in a rare blush. "I like the sound of that, but tell me now what's on your mind."

"Well, I guess I could do that. First we'll hit the beach with our boards, catch some waves. And after that skydiving and possibly some rock climbing, of course. Then I thought maybe we'd take in a movie and dinner and go home to get a little more intimate."

He chuckled over her bemused reaction. He kissed her lightly on the lips, and then once again before he continued his answer.

"Dinner still stands. I was going to ask you at dinner how you'd feel about getting married on the beach. I know of a secluded beach in Hawaii where we can drink Pomegranate Martinis and make love in the warm sand as long as we want. And since you've never known what a real family feels like, I was thinking …" He paused to brush a tear falling just below her eye. "Maybe we can start our own soon."

"Shane," she whispered as the very breath was stolen from her.

"I love you, Haley," he whispered back. "I used to believe my badge meant more to me than anything, but that's changed. And there's no doubt in my mind exactly what I want." He gazed into her eyes. "I'm not much of a superhero, but what do you say? Want to get married?"

She slid her arms around his neck and kissed him tenderly on the lips. "The world has plenty of heroes, Shane," she said gazing at him with pleading eyes. "I just need one." She pulled away with a genuine grin, and then raised her pinky before him. "I promised you a pinky swear a long time ago. It's about time I gave it to you."

He took her pinky and then grinned as he pulled her into his arms. "Does this mean you're mine?"

"Yes," she replied.

"Can I arrest you every night?"

She laughed. "Sure, why not?"

"Handcuffs?"

"Maybe."

"What about a rematch?"

"Oh," she laughed. "I don't think you want to lose again."

He chuckled as she took his face in her hands and massaged gently.

She kissed him lightly on the lips. "I want to be with you always," she whispered and kissed him once more.

"That's the sexiest thing I've ever heard," he whispered back as he stared deeply into her eyes.

"Then take me home," she said, then whispered again in his ear, "I want to be with you now."

"And I stand corrected."

•••

Angela Steed

Born in Seattle, Washington, the author grew up in a small town on the Oregon Coast. After living in Portland, Oregon, she moved to the beautiful Appalachian Mountains of West Virginia where she lives with her husband and two daughters. In addition to being a novelist, Angela is a licensed realtor, freelance writer and computer specialist.

www.AngelaSteed.com

Also by this author ...

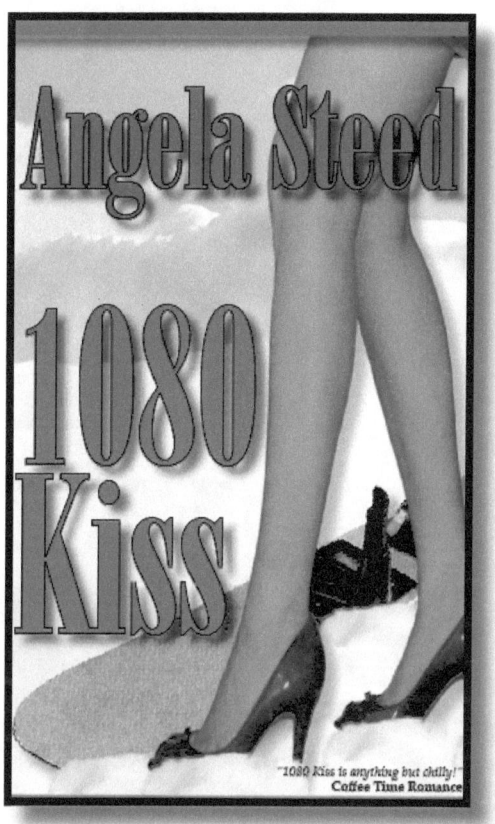

Angela Steed

1080 Kiss

"1080 Kiss is anything but chilly!"
Coffee Time Romance

The "God of Snow" has met his match.

Professional snowboarder Vince Evans, "The God of Snow," has met his match in public relations extraordinaire Morgan Price. But will she break the rules of business for this black haired, green eyed bad-boy-turned-good?

Author of 1080 Kiss

ANGELA STEED

The Sea's Embrace

During a museum excursion, a controversial
relic is pulled from the ocean depths contain-
ing a mystery to which Katherine is inexpli-
cably joined. Born of the old gods, punished
and locked away, Derrick has crossed seas of
time to find Katherine, until an unthinkable
decision threatens everything.